Fee Fie Fo Fun

Enchanting Fairy Tale Units for Busy Teachers of Young Children

Carol Taylor Bond

Edited by Joyce Beecher King

Published by PP PARTNER PRESS INC.
Box 124
Livonia, MI 48152

ISBN 0-933212-34-8

Distributed by:

Gryphon House
3706 Otis Street
Mt. Rainier, Maryland 20822

To my mother,

Dolores W. Close

and

To my grandmother,

Lottie S. Griffith

Acknowledgements

I wish to thank the following people for their inspiration and support: Charlotte Murchison; Susan Myrick; my husband, Brantley; my children, Amy, Scott, and Destin; friends and students at Ruby-Wise Elementary, Kolin, Louisiana; the helpful staff of the Rapides Parish Public Library, Alexandria, Louisiana; and all my family and friends for their continued encouragement.

I gratefully acknowledge the authors and publishers listed below, for granting permission to reprint materials in this book. Every effort has been made to trace the ownership and to acknowledge the use of materials not written by the author. If any error inadvertently occurred, please notify the publisher for corrections in future editions.

Liz Cromwell and Dixie Hibner for use of the peanut butter recipe from Explore and Create, published by Partner Press, Box 124, Livonia, Michigan 48152.

Table of Contents

Introduction. vi

How to Use the Book vi

Room Environment 1

    Patterns, Pictures, Etc. 4

Little Red Riding Hood 10

    Patterns, Pictures, Etc. 16

Hansel and Gretel 27

    Patterns, Pictures, Etc. 33

Snow White and the Seven Dwarfs 41

    Patterns, Pictures, Etc. 47

Jack and the Beanstalk 54

    Patterns, Pictures, Etc. 62

Dumbo of the Circus 67

    Patterns, Pictures, Etc. 76

Cinderella 86

    Patterns, Pictures, Etc. 93

Goldilocks and the Three Bears 102

    Patterns, Pictures, Etc. 108

Peter Pan 121

    Patterns, Pictures, Etc. 128

The Wolf and the Seven Kids 136

    Patterns, Pictures, Etc. 143

Bibliography 155

Index 156

Introduction

Fairy tales have always held a special fascination for children as well as adults. In fairy tales, the listener escapes to a world where everyday life is less complicated. The characters are simple—either good or bad, and they are easily identified with. The plots are fast-moving, and the language is rhythmic. Usually some type of magic is used to right the wrongs and, in the end, the good are rewarded and the bad swiftly punished.

Fee Fie Fo Fun provides instructional units based on favorite fairy tales. Each unit contains multiple activities designed to teach basic skills to children ages four to seven. Included are step-by-step directions for all activities, words, and actions for fingerplays and songs, ready-made worksheets, patterns, illustrations of finished projects, letters to parents, and recipes.

How to Use the Book

The format of Fee Fie Fo Fun, detailed below, is similar to the teacher's daily lesson plan. Each unit is arranged with the classroom schedule in mind and, in addition, offers several activities for each subject. The teacher, therefore, chooses the most appropriate activity in terms of student ability levels, time allotments, availability of materials, and personal preferences. The units themselves may be taught individually or presented in succession.

Room Environment - The room environment "sets the stage" for presenting the units. It includes directions for making a backdrop for the story area, a display table, decorations for the ceiling, a prop box, and three bulletin boards. Most of these can be made with the children's assistance and/or artwork. Illustrated examples can be found in the Patterns, Pictures, Etc. section following this portion of the book.

Source - Since there are numerous versions of particular fairy tales, the title of the book used to develop each unit is found below the unit title. Young children respond better to fairy tales with more pictures and less text. The versions used were chosen with this in mind. You may read or tell the story as desired.

<u>Language Arts - Social Studies - Science</u> - This section offers a variety of activities to further develop the unit concept. Corresponding ready-made worksheets and patterns are found in the Patterns, Pictures, Etc. section following each unit.

<u>Before the Story</u> - Before the Story explains necessary preparations for the story. These include displays to introduce the story, demonstrations to be used during the story, and the setting up of activities to be completed after the story.

<u>Vocabulary Words</u> - The vocabulary words are taken from the particular source used to develop the unit (see "Source" above). These will vary according to the fairy tale version you use. The words may be listed on the board and defined before the story or defined during the story by offering an alternative word.

<u>After the Story</u> - This section contains a variety of activities to promote further understanding and enjoyment of the story. Necessary patterns and illustrated examples are found in the Patterns, Pictures, Etc. section following each unit.

<u>Art</u> - The Art section offers art activities employing various methods and materials. Since many of the projects require some use of patterns, encourage creativity whenever possible. Allow the children to choose preferred colors, design methods, and materials whenever possible. At a separate time each day, set up an art center for small groups. Include easels and painting materials, clay, scrap paper, scissors, glue, crayons, etc. This practice promotes creativity with few restrictions. Patterns and illustrated examples of activities are found in the Patterns, Pictures, Etc. section following each unit.

<u>Math</u> - The Math section provides nonsequential activities to teach basic skills such as counting, spatial concepts, one-to-one correspondence, and so forth. Ready-made worksheets are found in the Patterns, Pictures, Etc. section following each unit.

<u>Music - Movement - Games</u> - Music - Movement - Games includes songs, movement activities, and games. Many of the songs are sung to the tunes of popular songs as indicated.

Fairy Tale Kitchen - Fairy Tale Kitchen offers recipes for cooking activities. To present the activity, it is a good idea to write the recipe on the chalkboard or experience chart paper, illustrating each ingredient. Below this, draw and label the utensils to be used to prepare the recipe. Spread the utensils and ingredients on a covered table. Read the recipe aloud. Identify and discuss the items on the table. Pass around samples of the ingredients, encouraging the children to describe the appearance, taste, feel, and smell of each. When preparing the recipe, allow the children to participate as much as possible.

Patterns, Pictures, Etc. - This section follows the Room Environment section and each unit, and includes pictures of bulletin boards, displays, and art projects, patterns, ready-made worksheets, and letters to parents.

DISPLAYS

Story Area Backdrop

Obtain a corrugated cardboard refrigerator box. Cut away the top and bottom and cut at one corner to open. Use markers or tempera paint to make a castle on one side of the box and a house on the other. (See examples on page 4.) Stand this backdrop in the Story Area so that the children face it when you are reading the stories. For stories including a castle, display the castle side; for those including a house or cottage, display the house side. When indicated, add extra features to the castle or house. For example, attach construction paper candy for the witch's house in Hansel and Gretel.

Display Table

Set a table in front of the backdrop. Cover with a sheet of white bulletin board paper. Cut stars and moons from gold wrapping paper and glue on the paper tablecloth. Or, purchase material with a fairy tale design and cut with pinking sheers to make a tablecloth. Use the table to display items related to the story, story books, and so forth.

Note: Purchased stickers of moons and stars may be used to decorate the paper tablecloth.

Ceiling Decorations

Enlarge the patterns on page 5 and use to make stars and crescent moons to hang from the ceiling. Make a cardboard pattern of each and trace on tagboard or poster paper. Punch holes at the tops. Cover with glue and sprinkle with gold glitter. Attach fishing line and hang from the ceiling over the Story Area or all around the room.

Wall Display - "Climbing the Beanstalk"

Make a large beanstalk from green bulletin board paper. Cut the stalk and leaves and tape to the wall. Make a cloud from white paper. Write the title on the cloud and tape at the top of the beanstalk. Display the children's worksheets and artwork by mounting on the leaves. (See example on page 6.)

Prop Box

Paint a large corrugated cardboard box to resemble a treasure chest, or cover with contact paper and decorate as desired. Fill with dress-up clothes and costumes, hats of all kinds, magic wands, toy swords, crowns, etc.   The children use these at Activity Time for role-playing or in dramatizations of individual fairy tales.

Note: Secondhand clothes from older children work especially well. Adult clothing usually requires hemming.

BULLETIN BOARDS

"Fairy Tale Fun"

Cover and trim the bulletin board with pastel colors. Staple the title at the top. Enlarge the pattern on page 7 to make the top of a castle. The castle should be the width of the bulletin board. Mount directly above the bulletin board. Use the bulletin board space to display daily artwork, such as "Cinderella's Coach" (page 89), "Hansel's Prison" (page 30), and "Padded Poison Apples" (page 43). (See example on page 8.)

"When You Wish Upon a Star"

Cover the bulletin board with royal blue paper and trim with a green border. Using the pattern on page 5, make a yellow construction paper star for each child. Discuss wishing on a star and ask the class, "If you had one wish, what would it be?" Distribute the stars. The children draw their wishes on the stars or cut out pictures of their wishes from magazines and glue them on the stars. The wishes should be labeled by the children (or teacher) with their names included. Mount the stars on the bulletin board. (See example on page 9.)

"And They Lived Happily Ever After"

Cover and trim the bulletin board as desired. Staple the title at the top. Draw, color, and cut out characters from each fairy tale that "lived happily ever after," such as Cinderella and the Prince; Jack and his family ("Jack and the Beanstalk"); Hansel and Gretel and their father; and Little Red Riding Hood, her mother, and grandmother. Staple the main characters on either side of the bulletin board and the matching character or characters (with a stick pin beside them) on the opposite side. Cut pieces of yarn long enough to extend between the pictures and attach a paper clip to one end of each piece. Bend one end of the paper clip outward to form a hook. Staple the ends (without paper clips) next to the main characters. The children find the characters that match, extend the yarn between them, and place the paper clip hook over the stick pin. (See example on page 9.)

Note: Pictures of characters may be drawn with the aid of an overhead projector or may be cut from fairy tale coloring books.

Story Area Backdrop

one side of display

other side of display

Ceiling Decorations · Patterns

Climbing the Beanstalk

Wall Display

Fairy Tale Fun- Bulletin Board Pattern

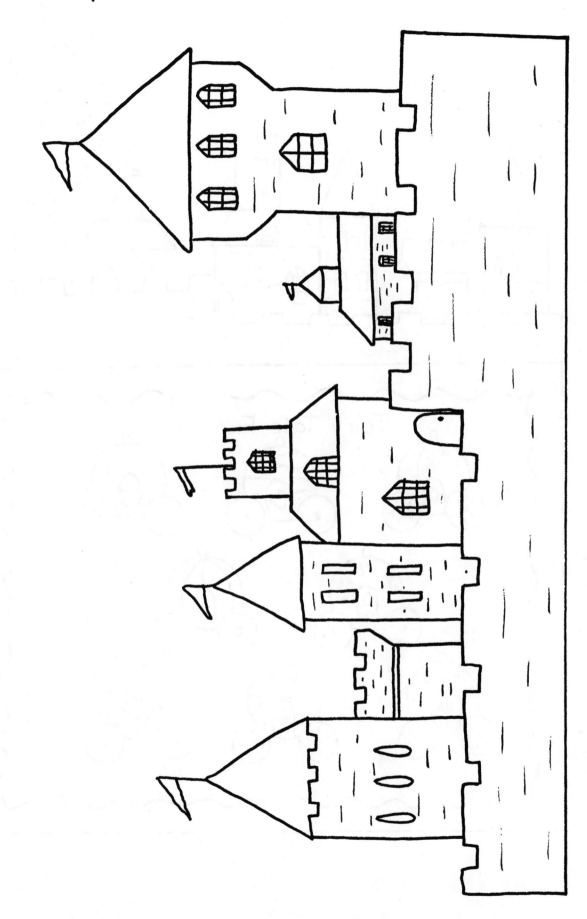

Bulletin Boards

Fairy Tale Fun

LITTLE RED RIDING HOOD

Source: <u>Little Red Riding Hood</u> by the Brothers Grimm with pictures by
Harriet Pincus

LANGUAGE ARTS - SOCIAL STUDIES - SCIENCE

Before the Story

Send home the parents' letter on page 16, if desired. Make a red riding
hood for a doll by cutting a square of red tissue paper or material. Place
the middle of one edge on the doll's head and gather at the neck and tie
with yarn. Put the doll, a basket, a jar of honey, a bouquet of real or
artificial flowers, a picture of some muffins, a pair of scissors, a stuffed
or plastic wolf (or picture of a wolf), and some rocks in a paper sack.
One by one, remove the objects from the sack and have the children
identify them. Put the objects on the Display Table. Announce the name
of the story. Tell the children to listen carefully and determine what part
each of these things play in the story.

Vocabulary Words

maid	wicked	huntsman
hood	hazelnut trees	snips
velvet	nosegay	fetched
ill	latch	wander
village	gulp	

After the Story

Ask the children to recall the events of the story as you record them on
experience chart paper. Leave a space after each sentence for the
children to illustrate each event.

Red Day

A few days in advance, send home the parents' letter on "Red Day" (see
page 17). On this day, the children should wear red clothing and bring
one red object from home. Have each child stand while the others
identify the red clothing he or she is wearing. Then ask the children to
share the red objects brought from home. Brainstorm for "things that are
red" and list on the chalkboard. Read a book such as <u>I Like Red</u> by Marie

Norkin Warach, or <u>Clifford, the Big Red Dog</u> by Norman Bridwell. Let the children make a red mural by cutting out red pictures from old magazines and gluing on mural paper. Sing a song such as "Little Red Caboose" and serve a red snack such as strawberries or cherries. Play "I Spy" using red objects only.

Visual Discrimination Activity

Obtain a sample book of different fabrics from an upholstery store. Cut two 2" x 3" strips of each material including red velvet (the material of the red riding hood). Vary the colors and textures so that the pairs are different from each other. Glue each strip onto separate 3" x 5" index cards. Seat the students in a circle. Separate the pairs, giving one card (of each pair) to each student. Spread out the remaining cards in the center of the circle. Discuss the distinguishing characteristics of the various fabric strips. Choose a child to go to the center of the circle and place his or her card on top of the matching card. Continue in this manner, proceeding around the circle, until all cards are matched. Place in a box to be used as an individual learning game at Activity Time.

Fingerplay - "Little Red Riding Hood's Tale"

That looks like Grandma's nightgown, (Put hands on shoulders)

That looks like Grandma's cap, (Form circle with hands, place on head)

That looks like my dear Grandma

As she takes her morning nap. (Eyes closed, hands together
                                              next to cheek)

But those aren't Grandma's ears (Touch ears)

And those aren't Grandma's eyes, (Point to eyes)

Those aren't Grandma's teeth—Help! Help! (Bare teeth, hands in air)

But Grandma's here inside! (Point finger)

Oh, I think I hear the hunter, (Cup hand behind ear)

Oh, I know I hear a shout, (Cup hand behind ear)

And now I hear the scissors—Snip! Snip! (Make cutting motions with
                                                        pointer and middle fingers)

Oh, the hunter has let us out! (Climb out)

Now Grandma's eating cakes and honey, (Pretend to eat)

And I am eating bread, (Pretend to eat)

But the hunter has filled the wolf with stones,   (Make circle with arms
                                            to show big stomach)

And now he is quite dead!   (Close eyes, stick out tongue)

Little Red Riding Hood Maze

Duplicate and distribute the sheet on page 18. The children draw the path
to Grandma's house as directed, then color the pictures.

Going to Grandma's - Alphabet Game and Follow-Up

On a sheet of poster paper, enlarge and draw the game board on page 19.
Color the squares different colors. Divide the class into two teams and
place a marker (small block or toy) for each team at the start. Select a
player from one team to start the game. Hold up a flashcard of the letter
A. The player says, "I am going to Grandma's with an _____ (the
student supplies an **A** word) in my basket." If the player is unable to
think of an **A** word, he or she may consult with the team. If he or she is
successful, the team's marker is moved to the next square. If not, the
marker remains on the same square and a volunteer from the other team
can supply an **A** word.

For the next turn, choose a player from the other team and repeat the
procedure but hold up the **B** flashcard. The player must supply a word
beginning with the letter **B** to complete the sentence. Continue in this
manner, alternating teams and proceeding through the alphabet until a
team reaches Grandma's house and wins the game.

Follow-Up: For each child, make a paper plate basket by cutting out part
of the center as shown on page 20. Write a different alphabet letter on
each plate. Distribute along with old magazines, scissors, and glue. The
children cut out pictures of things beginning with the correct letters and
glue onto their "baskets."

ART

The Wolf's X-Rays

Preparation - Duplicate and distribute the sheets on pages 21 and 22.
Provide crayons, glue, and scissors.

Procedure - Color the wolf with the side of a crayon and cut out. Color
Grandma and Little Red Riding Hood in the normal fashion but press

harder to make dark strokes. Cut out on the dotted lines. Spread a thin layer of glue to cover (the front of) Grandma and Little Red Riding Hood. Glue to the middle back of the wolf's body section. Hold the wolf in front of a light to see what's inside. (See example on page 20.)

Paper Weave Baskets

Preparation - Duplicate the pattern (see page 23) on manila paper. Cut various colors of construction paper into strips 2" x 10". Give each child the pattern sheet, one of the strips (color of their choice), scissors, crayons, and glue.

Procedure - Cut out and color the basket, the jar of honey, and the cakes. Bend the basket on the dotted line and make a small cut on each solid line. Unbend, insert one blade of the scissors, and cut on the solid line in each direction. Be sure to stop at each end of the lines. Cut the strip in half lengthwise to make two 1" x 10" strips. Beginning at the bottom of the basket, weave one strip over and under, over and under the sections of the basket. Weave the next strip under and over, under and over the sections of the basket. To secure the ends, dab with glue and trim the excess. Turn the basket over. Glue on the cakes and the jar of honey so that they show above the top. (See example on page 20.)

The Hungry Wolf

Preparation - Duplicate the pattern sheet (see page 24) on white construction paper and distribute. Provide a metal paper fastener for each child. Set out crayons, scissors, and glue.

Procedure - Color the wolf's head and the hat and tongue (below the dotted line on the handle section). Cut out each section. Insert the paper fastener through the dot on the wolf's head, then through the dot on the handle section. Turn over and spread apart the ends of the fastener. Hold the wolf's head and move the hat from side to side. The wolf's tongue will wiggle. (See example on page 20.)

MATH

Filling the Wolf with Stones

Duplicate the sheet on page 25. Write a different number in the blank on each sheet. Lead the class outside and direct the children to collect a handful of pebbles. Inside, place the pebbles on paper plates, and distribute the sheets, crayons, and glue. The children color the wolves, then glue the indicated number of pebbles inside the stomach area of each. Direct the children to place each pebble in a "puddle" of glue. Dry thoroughly.

Arranging Flowers - Activity and Sheet

Duplicate the sheet on page 26 and set aside. Place real or artificial flowers in a vase with an empty vase beside it. Select a child to find the shortest flower in the arrangement and move it to the other vase. Choose another child to find the tallest flower and move it to the other vase. Repeat each direction until all flowers are moved to the other vase. Hand out the duplicated sheet along with a sheet of white unlined paper. The children color and cut out the flowers on the dotted lines, then glue from left to right in order of heights (shortest to tallest) on the white unlined paper.

Note: If desired, draw a star on the left side of each sheet of the white unlined paper to show the children where to begin gluing the flowers.

MUSIC - MOVEMENT - GAMES

Song - "Mean and Hungry People-Eater"

Tune: "One-Eyed, One-Horned, Flying Purple People-Eater"

I'm the big bad wolf and I'm a mean and hungry people-eater,

Big bad wolf and I'm a mean and hungry people-eater,

Big bad wolf and I'm a mean and hungry people-eater,

Better watch out for me!

Movement - "Trail to Grandma's"

Make a winding trail on the classroom floor using masking tape. Using the footprint pattern on page 20, make footprints of various colors from construction paper. Label "left" and "right." Color, cut out, laminate if desired, and tape along the trail. The children walk on the trail in single file, placing their left and right feet on the correct footprints. Repeat the procedure, directing the children to hop on alternating feet, trot, walk "duck fashion," and run along the trail.

Note: If necessary, before the activity, write "left" and "right" on the chalkboard and discuss. Tie a piece of yarn around each child's right leg.

Game - "Grandma's Garb"

Obtain two ladies' nightgowns or robes, two pairs of ladies' slippers, and two hair nets or scarves. Place a complete "outfit" in each of two large paper sacks. Divide the class into two teams. The members of each team stand side by side in a line. The teams face each other with four or five feet between them. Give a sack of clothing to the first player (either end) in each line. Put a record on the record player. When the music begins, the players on each team pass their sacks up and down the line. Pick up the arm of the record player. When the music stops, the players holding the sacks must open them and put on the clothes as quickly as possible. The player who finishes first wins that round, or a point if you wish to keep score, for his or her team. Continue in this manner for a specified number of rounds, or until the children lose interest.

FAIRY TALE KITCHEN

Tiny Apple Cakes

2 cups sugar
1 1/2 teaspoons soda
1 teaspoon salt
3 cups flour
1 cup vegetable oil
2 eggs, beaten
2 teaspoons vanilla
3 cups apples, cubed
1/4 cup milk

Preheat oven to 350°. Grease small muffin tins. Sift dry ingredients and set aside. Mix oil, eggs, vanilla, apples, and milk. Add to dry ingredients, mixing well. Fill muffin tins almost to the tops. Bake 20-25 minutes or until light golden brown. Serve topped with honey if desired. Yield: 72 1½" muffins.

Variation: Purchase a muffin mix. Prepare as directed.

Dear Parents,

On _____, our class will share the fairy tale "Little Red Riding Hood." The day's lessons and activities will center around this fairy tale. Please read below for ways you can help.

Things to send: _____
_____
_____

Volunteers needed to: _____
_____
_____

Follow-up Activities: Ask your child to share the following songs,
games, and other activities related to the fairy
tale:

_____
_____
_____

Ask your child the following questions about the fairy tale:
_____
_____
_____

Thank you for your cooperation.

Sincerely,

Dear Parents,

    On _____, our class will read the fairy tale "Little Red Riding Hood." On this day, in conjunction with the story, we will have "Red Day."

For "Red Day," I am asking that the children wear at least one article of red clothing (more if possible) and bring one red object from home. The object should not be breakable or valuable and should be placed in a paper bag labeled with your child's name. It will be returned at the end of the day.

Besides sharing the red objects and observing the red clothing, we will have the following activities to teach the color red:

_____

_____

_____

    Thank you for your cooperation.

              Sincerely,

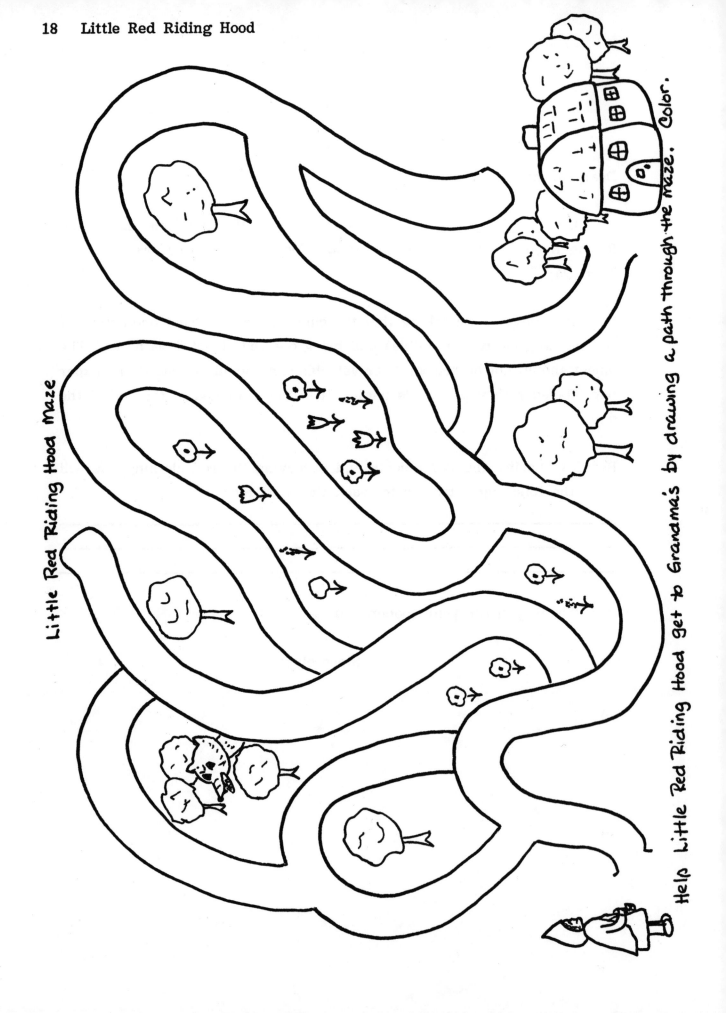

Little Red Riding Hood Maze

Help Little Red Riding Hood get to Grandma's by drawing a path through the maze. Color.

Going to Grandma's - Alphabet Game
Game Board

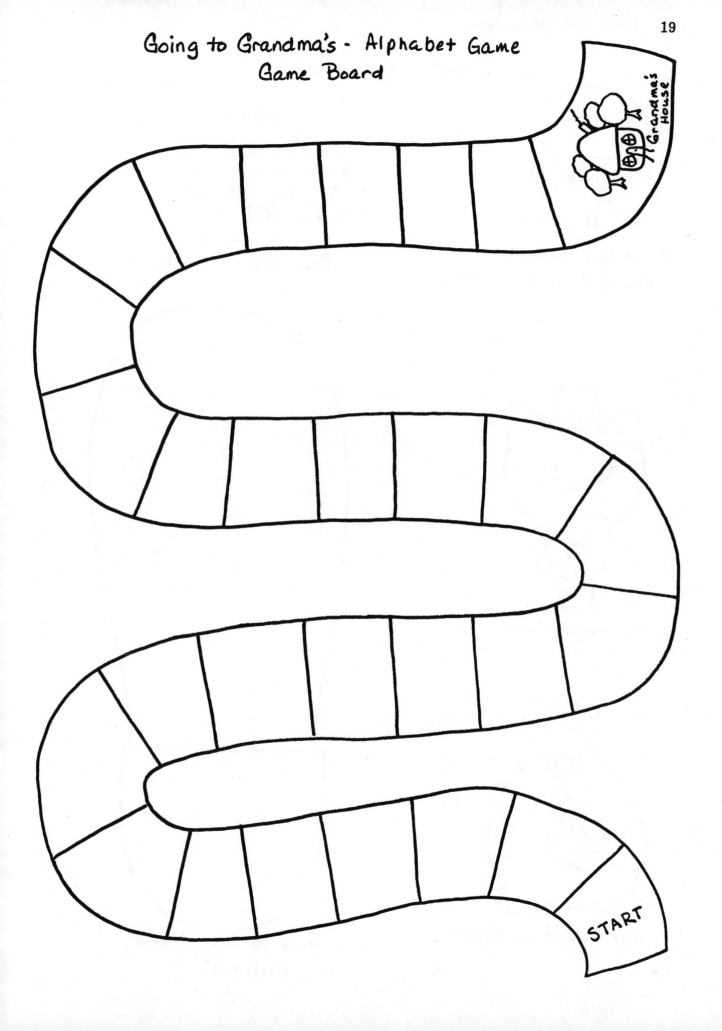

Grandma's House

START

Examples, Patterns

Going to Grandma's -
Alphabet Game Follow-Up

Paper Weave Baskets

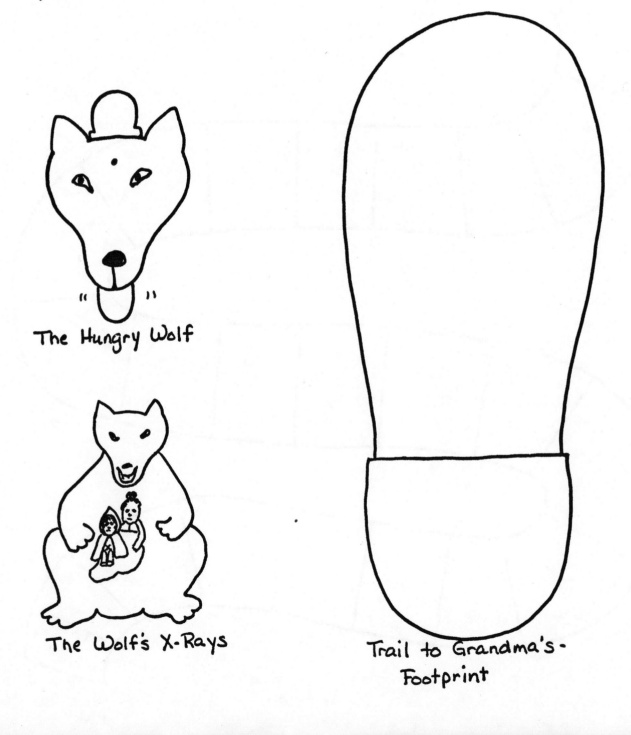

The Hungry Wolf

The Wolf's X-Rays

Trail to Grandma's -
Footprint

The Wolf's X-Rays

The Wolf's X-Rays

Paper Weave Baskets
Patterns

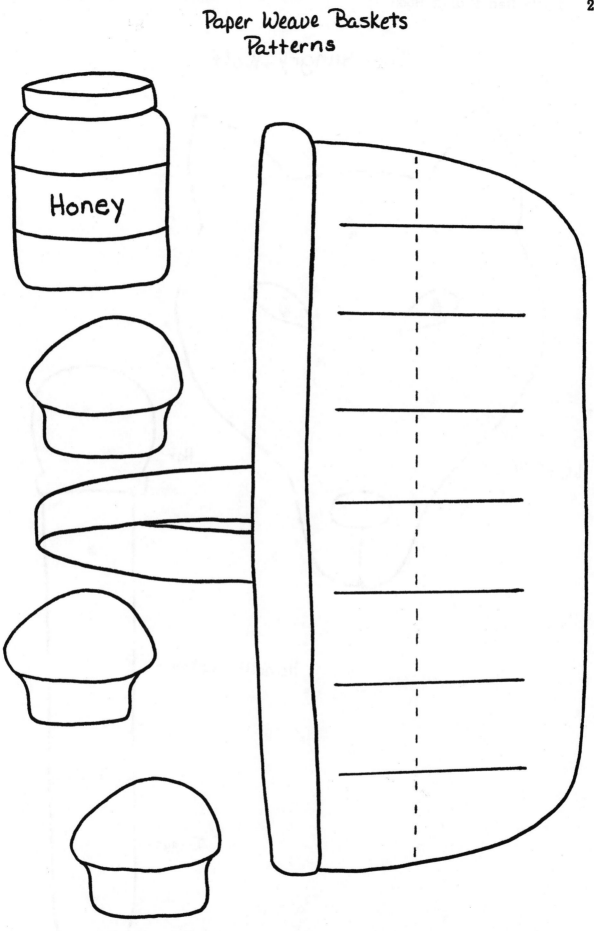

The Hungry Wolf

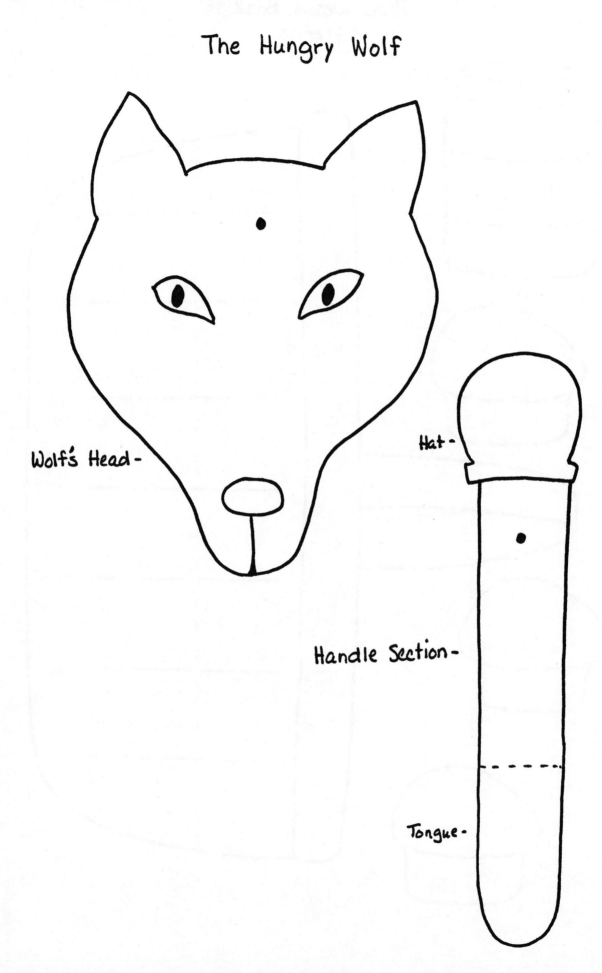

Wolf's Head -

Hat -

Handle Section -

Tongue -

Filling the Wolf With Stones

Arranging Flowers

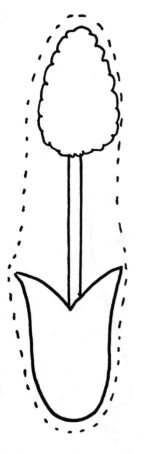

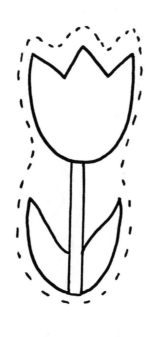

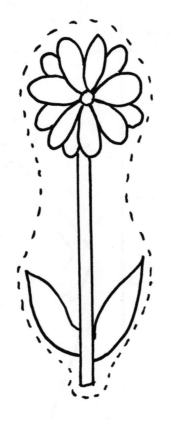

HANSEL AND GRETEL

Source: Hansel and Gretel, by the Brothers Grimm, illustrated by Arnold Lobel

LANGUAGE ARTS - SOCIAL STUDIES - SCIENCE

Before the Story

Send home the parents' letter on page 33, if desired. Make a "Story Yarn" by cutting a piece of yarn long enough to be held by all the children as they sit in a circle. String a medium-sized bead on the yarn and tie a bead to each end. Set aside. Use masking tape to make a path on the floor which winds and loops around the classroom and ends at the Story Area. When it is time to begin the story, the children follow the path in single file to the Story Area.

Vocabulary Words

dwelt	bough	ancient
woodcutter	fatigue	sumptuous
famine	conscience	stable
beasts	reproached	perish
daybreak	transparent	hag
farewell	casement	precious stones

After the Story

Seat the children in the circle with each child holding a portion of the "Story Yarn." Slide the loose bead to one end of the yarn. The child at that end will hold the bead and will be the first to speak. Direct the children to retell the story of Hansel and Gretel. Using one complete sentence, the first child tells the beginning of the story, then slides the bead to the second child. The second child uses a complete sentence to tell what happened next in the story, then slides the bead to the third child, and so forth. Continue until the story is completed.

Rhyming Words

Draw a large gingerbread house on poster paper. Color and cut out. Using old magazines and workbooks, find and cut out pictures of the following: a loaf of bread, a girl, a boy, a pebble, a tree, a house, a bird,

a witch, a bone, a duck, and a pearl.   Glue on the gingerbread house.
Read each sentence below.   The children listen to the sentence, then find
the rhyming word pictured on the gingerbread house.

1. I rhyme with said.   I'm a loaf of _ _ _ _ .   (bread)
2. I rhyme with twirl.   I'm a _ _ _ _ . (girl)
3. I rhyme with toy.   I'm a _ _ _ . (boy)
4. I rhyme with rebel.   I'm a _ _ _ _ _ _ . (pebble)
5. I rhyme with bee.   I'm a _ _ _ _ . (tree)
6. I rhyme with mouse.   I'm a _ _ _ _ _ . (house)
7. I rhyme with heard.   I'm a _ _ _ _ . (bird)
8. I rhyme with ditch.   I'm a _ _ _ _ _ . (witch)
9. I rhyme with stone.   I'm a _ _ _ _ . (bone)
10. I rhyme with luck.   I'm a _ _ _ _ . (duck)
11. I rhyme with curl.   I'm a _ _ _ _ _ . (pearl)

Demonstration

Ask a parent to visit the class and demonstrate making bread.

Character Shout

Divide the class into five groups.   Teach one of the character's lines
(below) to each group.   Let the groups practice their lines.   To begin,
raise your hand to signal the groups to recite their lines softly.   The
groups will be reciting all at one time.   Raise your hand a little higher for
the groups to recite the lines again and slightly increase the volume.
Continue in this manner until all groups are shouting their lines.

Father: "It's no joke, we are broke!"

Stepmother: "Get rid of those kids!"

Hansel and Gretel: "On our own away from home!"

Witch: "Let me feel, my next meal!"

Duck: "Quack, quack, ride on my back!"

Hansel and Gretel Alphabet Activity

Using the patterns on page 34, enlarge and transfer to poster paper. Cut
out. Ask the students to identify each figure and the alphabet letter it
begins with.   Write the beginning letter in the middle of each figure.
Divide the class into four groups and distribute the figures. Provide old
magazines and catalogs, scissors, and crayons. The students find pictures

of things beginning with the same letters, cut them out, and glue onto the figures. Display on a wall of the classroom.

Flannel Board Activity - "How Do They Feel?"

Use pellon or felt to make the patterns on page 35. Place on the flannel board. Discuss emotions and things that make us feel happy, sad, afraid, and angry. Place the different faces at the bottom of the flannel board to show these feelings. Read each sentence below; then call on a child to show the feeling involved by placing the correct face in the middle of the flannel board. (The face will represent the subject of each sentence.)

1. Hansel was playing with his kitten.
2. Gretel heard her stepmother saying mean things.
3. Hansel saw that the birds had eaten the bread crumbs.
4. Gretel saw a house of gingerbread.
5. The witch discovered the children eating her house.
6. Hansel saw a witch come out of the house.
7. Hansel was locked in the stable.
8. Gretel knew that the witch was going to eat her brother.
9. The witch was hungry, but Hansel wasn't fat enough.
10. The witch felt Gretel push her into the oven.
11. Gretel freed her brother.
12. Hansel and Gretel's father was alone thinking about his lost children.
13. Hansel and Gretel's father saw them walk through the door.
14. Hansel showed his father the pearls and precious stones.

ART

Gingerbread Houses

Preparation - Purchase macaroni and dried beans and peas. Dye the macaroni different colors by placing in bowls of food coloring mixed with water for a few minutes. Dry on paper towels. Set out the macaroni, dried beans and peas, scraps of rickrack and yarn, old buttons, and red glitter. Give each child a piece of construction paper (color of their choice). Provide crayons or markers, red glitter, glue, and scissors.

Procedure - Fold the sheet of construction paper in half to measure 6" x 9" and place in front of you with the fold at the top. To form the roof, make diagonal cuts to cut away the top two corners. Draw the door, windows, and roof. Open the sheet and draw a witch inside. To make the witch's red eyes, draw two circles, dab with glue, and sprinkle with red glitter. Dry. Use the macaroni, beans and peas, rickrack, etc., to decorate the front of the house.   Dry thoroughly.   (See example on page 36.)

Hansel's Prison

<u>Preparation</u> - Collect small styrofoam meat trays, one per child.   Cut pieces of black yarn long enough to wrap around and around the trays, as explained below.   Give each child a half-sheet of white construction paper, crayons, scissors, glue, a meat tray, and a piece of black yarn.

<u>Procedure</u> - On the white construction paper, draw and color Hansel.   Cut out and glue onto the meat tray.   Cut one slit near the top left corner of the meat tray and one slit near the bottom right corner.   Insert one end of the yarn in the top slit.   To form the prison bars, wrap around and around the tray, and insert the other end in the bottom slit.   Trim the ends.   (See example on page 36.)

Note: Some children may draw Hansel as a stick figure.   In this case, direct the children to cut around the figure in the shape of an oval or rectangle and glue it on the meat tray.

Woodcutter's Axe

<u>Preparation</u> - Duplicate the blade sheet (see page 37) on stiff, white construction paper.   Cut sheets of brown construction paper in half to measure 4½" x 12".   Tear 10" x 12" sheets of aluminum foil, two per child. Give each child a blade sheet, a half-sheet of brown construction paper, and two sheets of aluminum foil.   Have staplers available.

<u>Procedure</u> - To make the handle, roll the half-sheet of brown construction paper into a tube, 12" long.   Press to flatten and staple at each end.   Cut out the blades.   Fold a piece of foil around each blade to cover.   Press with your fingers to mold the foil to the shape of the blades.   Staple the blades together at the left and right sides so that the raw edges of the aluminum foil are concealed.   Place the handle between the two blades. One end should extend about 3/4" above the top of the blades.   Staple the blades to the handle; then staple any remaining open edges.   (See example on page 36.)

MATH

The Witch's Jewels

Purchase sequins, seventeen per child. Duplicate and distribute the sheet on page 38. The students glue the indicated number of jewels (sequins) in each of Hansel's pockets as directed.

Gingerbread House Number Puzzle

Duplicate and distribute the two puzzle sheets on pages 39 and 40. The children cut out the puzzle pieces, count the pieces of candy on each, and glue in the correct place on the outline sheet. Once the glue has dried, the house can be colored.

MUSIC - MOVEMENT - GAMES

Action Song - "Run Away, Run Away"

Tune: "Frère Jacques" ("Are You Sleeping?")

Where is Hansel? (Hands behind back)

Where is Gretel? (Hands behind back)

We are lost; (Hold up left hand, wiggle first two fingers to talk)

We are lost! (Continue to wiggle two fingers to talk)

I'm the witch, I'll help you, (Hold up right hand, wiggle pointer finger to talk)

No you won't, you'll eat us, (Wiggle two fingers left hand)

Run away, run away. (Put left hand behind back, put right hand down)

Dance - "Hansel and Gretel"

Play a recording of the opera "Hansel and Gretel" by Engelbert Humperdinck. Teach the (self-explanatory) dance featured in the first act of the opera.

Game - "Nibble, Nibble"

Place penny candy in a paper sack. Seat the children in a semicircle. Choose a child to be the "Witch." The "Witch" sits in a chair in the middle of the semicircle holding the sack of candy and a die. The first child in the semicircle stands before the "Witch." The "Witch" says,

"Nibble, nibble, little mouse,
Who's that nibbling at my house?"

The child replies,

"It is _____ (name) and I must eat.
May I have a special treat?"

The "Witch" hands the child the die to roll on the floor, then gives the child the number of candies indicated on the die. Continue around the semicircle until everyone has a turn. Alternate "witches" if desired. When the game is completed, the children may eat the candy.

Variation: Substitute tokens for the candy. After the game, the children may use the tokens to "buy" the candy.

Note: You may wish to distribute additional candy so that all children have an equal amount.

Game - "Pebble Walk"

Fill a plastic bucket with pebbles. Choose one flat pebble and mark one side with a magic marker. Let the children choose partners and line up. The last two children carry the bucket of pebbles. The first two children in line take turns holding the marked pebble. Take a "Pebble Walk" around the school grounds. At each turn, stop and let the child with the marked pebble toss it in the air. When it lands, see which side is up. If it is the marked side, turn right; if it is the unmarked side, turn left. Meanwhile, the two children with the bucket should take turns dropping a pebble after every five steps. You may alternate children so that others get to toss the marked pebble and drop the pebbles from the bucket. When you run out of pebbles, follow the pebbles back to the classroom. Be sure to pick up the pebbles as you go.

FAIRY TALE KITCHEN

Gingerbread

2 1/2 cups flour
2 teaspoons baking soda
2 teaspoons ground ginger
1 teaspoon ground cinnamon
1/2 teaspoon ground cloves
1/2 teaspoon ground nutmeg
1/2 teaspoon baking powder

3 eggs, beaten
1/2 cup brown sugar
3/4 cup molasses
3/4 cup cooking oil
1 cup boiling water
Cool Whip

Preheat oven to 350°. Sift together dry ingredients and set aside. Mix beaten eggs, brown sugar, molasses, and oil. Combine with dry ingredients; then add boiling water. Mix thoroughly. Bake in a greased 9" x 13" x 2" pan for 25 minutes, or until top springs back when lightly touched. Serve with Cool Whip. Variation: Purchase and prepare gingerbread mix as directed. Serve with Cool Whip.

Dear Parents,

On _____, our class will share the fairy tale "Hansel and Gretel." The day's lessons and activities will center around this fairy tale. Please read below for ways you can help.

Things to send: _____
_____
_____

Volunteers needed to: _____
_____
_____

Follow-up Activities: Ask your child to share the following songs, games, and other activities related to the fairy tale:

_____
_____
_____

Ask your child the following questions about the fairy tale:

_____
_____
_____

Thank you for your cooperation.

Sincerely,

Hansel and Gretel Alphabet Activity

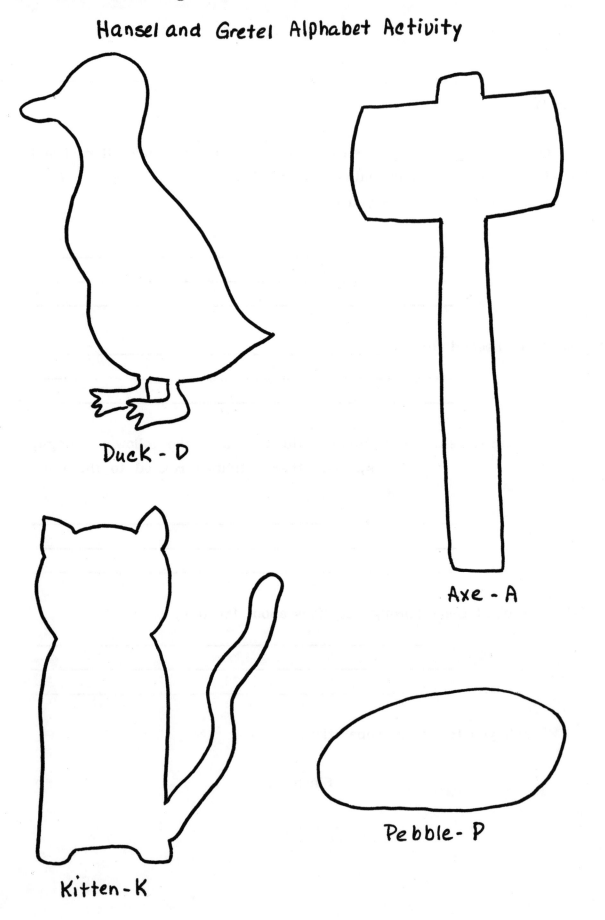

Duck - D

Axe - A

Kitten - K

Pebble - P

How Do They Feel? - Flannel Board Activity Patterns

Happy

Sad

Afraid

Angry

Examples

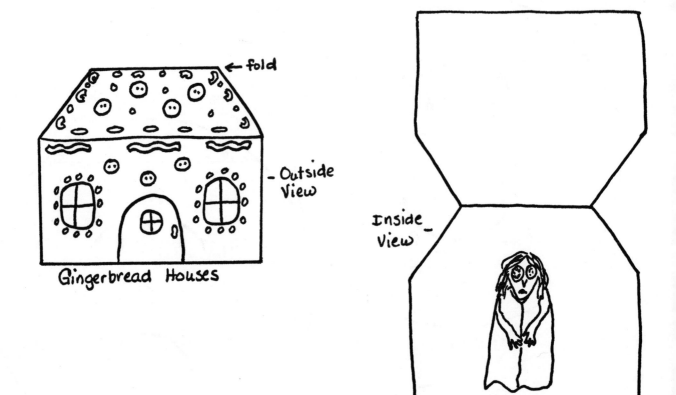

fold

Outside View

Gingerbread Houses

Inside View

Woodcutter's Axe

Hansel's Prison

Woodcutter's Axe

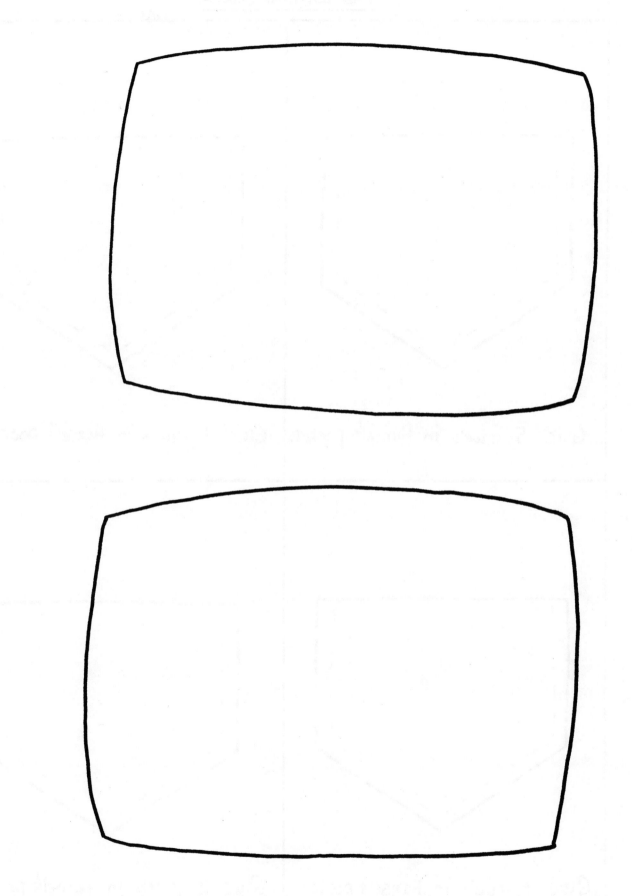

The Witch's Jewels

Name.

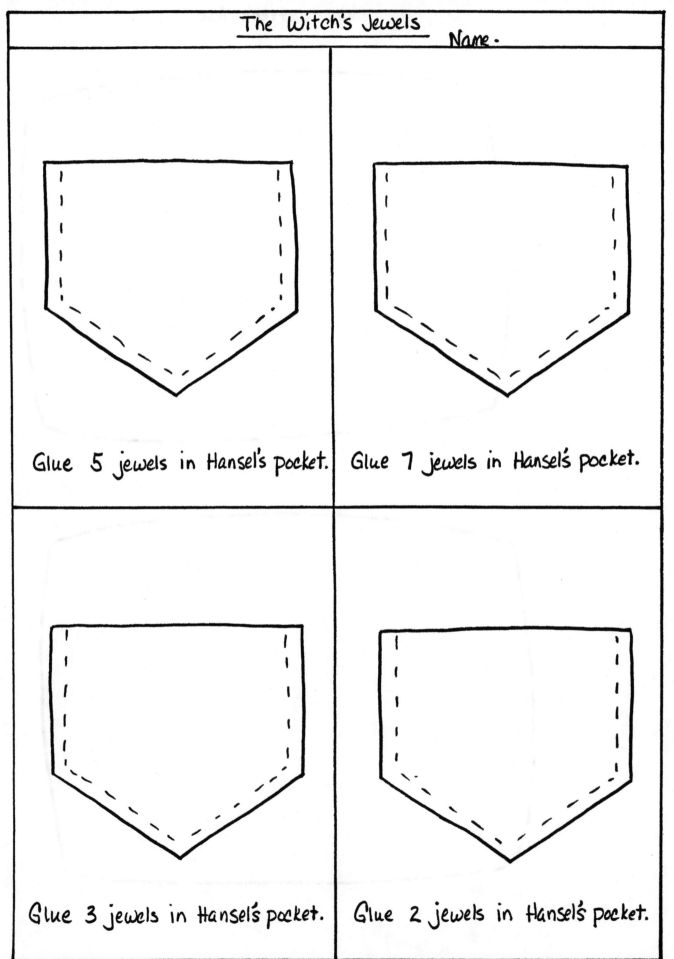

Glue 5 jewels in Hansel's pocket.

Glue 7 jewels in Hansel's pocket.

Glue 3 jewels in Hansel's pocket.

Glue 2 jewels in Hansel's pocket.

Gingerbread House Number Puzzle
Puzzle Pieces

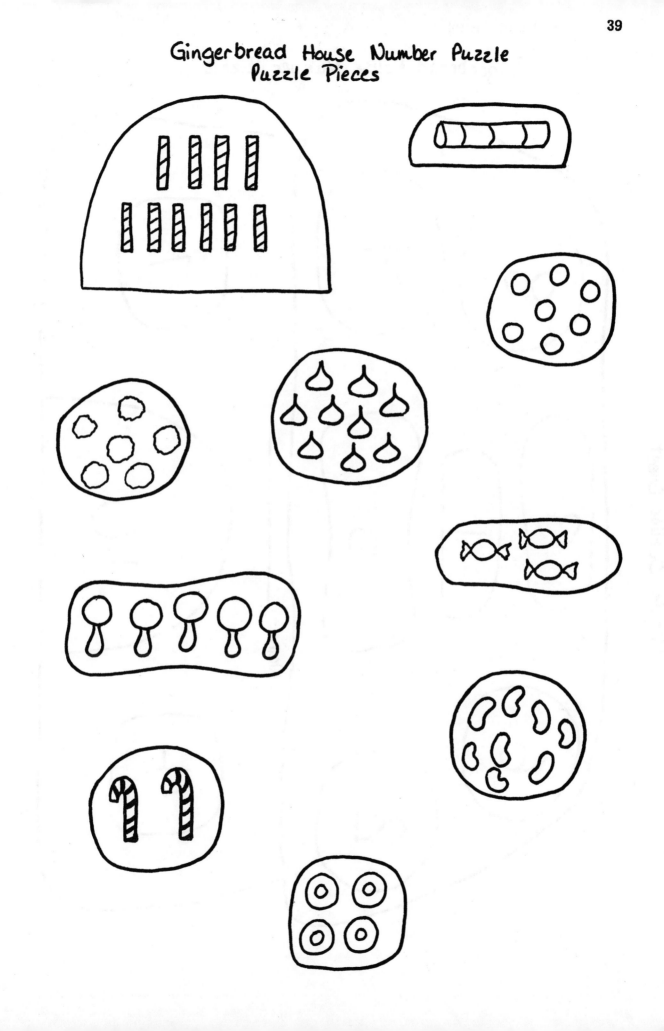

Gingerbread House Number Puzzle

Puzzle Outline Sheet

Name -

SNOW WHITE AND THE SEVEN DWARFS

Source: Walt Disney's Snow White and the Seven Dwarfs

LANGUAGE ARTS - SOCIAL STUDIES - SCIENCE

Before the Story

Send home the parents' letter on page 47, if desired. Make the stick puppets of Snow White, the seven dwarfs, the wicked stepmother, the stepmother as an old peddler woman, the huntsman, and the Prince (see Art). Place on the Display Table along with several apples, a can of apples (used for pie filling), a large bag of dried apples, a large jar of applesauce, a can of apple juice, and a hand mirror. Set up an opaque projector to display the illustrations as you read the story.

Vocabulary Words

kingdom	destroyed	dwarfs
vain	huntsman	mine
rivaled	merciful	concertina
jealous	persuaded	peddler
magic powers	deed	poisoned
envious	lurked	doom
dawn to dusk	cottage	lifeless
dreading	tidy	
ebony	spick-and-span	

After the Story

Give twelve children the puppets. Read the story again, letting the children use the puppets to act it out.

Apple Activity

Pass around the apples from the Display Table. Let the children feel, smell, and describe the apples. Slice the apples and give each child a piece to taste. Discuss texture and taste of the apples. Give each child a piece of dried apple to taste. Distribute small cups and plastic spoons. Pour a taste of apple juice into each cup. When the children have finished drinking the apple juice, spoon a taste of applesauce into each cup. Compare these different forms of apples. Discuss appearances and tastes and how each is made.

Name the Seven Dwarfs

Purchase alphabet noodles. Duplicate the Follow-Up sheet on page 48 and set aside. Discuss the names of the seven dwarfs. Ask the class, "If there was another dwarf, what would you name him?"; then give the following clues for each of the seven dwarfs' names. Call on volunteers to name the dwarf described in each clue. Write the answer on the board. Afterwards, complete the sheet as explained below.

1. Get out of my way, I'm coming through,
   I'm wearing a frown and a sullen look, too.
   I can vouch, I'm quite a grouch; I'm _ _ _ _ _ _. (Grumpy)

2. I sniffle and wheeze and say achoo,
   Over and over the whole day through.
   I must confess, my nose is a pest; I'm _ _ _ _ _ _. (Sneezy)

3. I'm always cheerful wherever I go,
   I do a little dance and say hello.
   I'm never mad, I'm always glad; I'm _ _ _ _ _. (Happy)

4. Oh, yawn, yawn, yawn, is it time for bed?
   Work or play—I'd rather snooze instead.
   It really feels lousy to be so drowsy; I'm _ _ _ _ _ _. (Sleepy)

5. I shuffle my feet and look at the floor;
   When folks are nice, I'm embarrassed even more.
   I don't know why I'm so shy; I'm _ _ _ _ _ _ _. (Bashful)

6. I don't heal the sick, despite my name,
   But I care for others just the same.
   I'm a friendly sort with a great big heart; I'm _ _ _. (Doc)

7. Sometimes I trip, sometimes I fall.
   I say silly things but I'm loved by all.
   I make people giggle when I give my ears a wiggle; I'm
   _ _ _ _ _. (Dopey)

Set out the alphabet noodles on paper plates. (If desired, display pictures of the seven dwarfs.) Distribute the Follow-Up sheets. Provide crayons or markers and glue. The students choose a dwarf and draw his head, arms, legs, etc., on the sheet. Next, they color the picture and put the dwarf's name on his shirt by gluing on the correct alphabet noodle letters.

Action Game - Snow White's Presents

The children stand side by side in a line facing the teacher. Ask them to repeat each line after you have read it, then imitate your actions (in parentheses). Each action should continue throughout the game.

One dwarf gave Snow White a pretty fan. (Fan yourself)

One dwarf gave Snow White a pair of scissors. (Make cutting motions
with other hand)

One dwarf gave Snow White a pogo stick. (Jump up and down)

One dwarf gave Snow White a baby doll. (Repeat "Mom-ma, Mom-ma")

Mirror Activities

Discuss the magic mirror in the story. Then, using a large hand mirror or
wall mirror, let the students take turns looking at themselves in the
mirror. Each student should describe himself or herself, then make faces
in the mirror for a few minutes to practice for the upcoming contest.
Have a "Making a Face in the Mirror" contest. Pass around the mirror
once again and let each student make the face he or she wishes to enter
in the contest. Put down the mirror and have all the students make the
same face once again. Award stickers to each child for the "scariest
face," "funniest face," "ugliest face," "meanest face," "grumpiest face", etc.,
so that each child gets a sticker.

ART

Snow White and the Seven Dwarfs Mural

Preparation - Provide a long sheet of mural paper, tempera paints, and
paintbrushes. Divide the class into small groups and assign a scene to
each group. Position the groups in order on one side of the mural paper.

Procedure - Discuss what you will paint with other group members. Paint
the scene on your section of the mural paper. Paint your name at the
bottom. (See example on page 49.)

Padded Poison Apples

Preparation - Use cardboard to make several patterns of the apple (see
page 50). Cut a 10" square of red bulletin board paper for each child.
Provide pencils, scissors, glue, and old newspapers. Have a stapler and a
staple remover available.

Procedure - Fold the sheet of red paper in half. Trace the pattern on
one side. Let the teacher staple the two layers together in the center of
the apple. Cut out the apple, cutting through both thicknesses. Remove
the staple. Except for three inches on one side, spread glue around the

edges of one apple. Place on top of the other apple to fit. Dry. Tear small pieces of newspaper and stuff through the opening to pad the apple. Staple along the opening. (See example on page 49.)

Stick Puppets

Preparation - Let each child choose the puppet he or she would like. Duplicate the patterns (see page 51) on stiff white construction paper and distribute. Give each child a wooden popsicle stick. Set out crayons, scissors, and staplers.

Procedure - Color the puppet and cut out on the dotted lines. Glue the popsicle stick to the back. Dry thoroughly.

Note: Enlarge the puppets using an opaque projector if desired.

Variation: Use strips of cardboard or straws instead of the popsicle sticks. Staple to the puppets.

MATH

Snow White Counting Sheet

Duplicate and distribute the sheet on page 52. Direct the children to count the objects in each block, circle the correct number below, then color the sheet.

Apple Trees

Purchase cranberries which will be used to represent tiny apples. Duplicate and distribute the sheet on page 53. The students color each tree, read the number below, and glue that many apples (cranberries) on the tree.

Variation: Set out red ink pads. The children make the correct number of fingerprint apples on the trees.

MUSIC - MOVEMENT - GAMES

Songs - "Whistle While You Work" and "Heigh Ho, Heigh Ho" by Larry Morey and Frank Churchill

Source: The Greatest Hits of Walt Disney (LP)

Dancing Dwarfs

Hang a large sheet of kraft paper across a corner of the room. Place a table in front of it. Draw the bodies of two dwarfs on the kraft paper. The dwarfs should be drawn so that their legs (which will be the arms of two children) will reach the table. Cut out holes for the heads, arms, and legs. Color the dwarfs' clothes. Choose four children to be the dwarfs. Two of the children get behind the paper, put socks and shoes on their hands, and place their heads in the large holes and their arms (the dwarfs' legs and feet) through the bottom holes. The other two children stand behind the first two children and put their arms under the first children's armpits and out through the top two holes to make the dwarfs' hands. Play a song on the record player (see songs above). The dwarfs sing the song, wave their arms, and dance on the table. Repeat, using different children.

Note: If you have difficulty drawing the dwarfs, place a picture of a dwarf on an opaque or overhead projector and project the picture on the kraft paper. Outline the dwarf; then color. Repeat for the second dwarf.

Movement - "Mirror Movements"

Ask the children to choose partners. One partner is the "Person" and one is the "Reflection." The "Person" makes various movements which the "Reflection" must attempt to follow. After a period of time, have the children change roles. Add music if desired.

Game - "Poison Apple"

The players form a circle with one player holding an apple. Play a record on the record player. When the music starts, the apple is passed around the circle. Stop the music. The player holding the apple when the music stops pretends to take a bite and then drops to the floor. That player then sits in the center of the circle and the game resumes. The last player standing gets to eat the (nonpoisonous!) apple.

FAIRY TALE KITCHEN

Baked Apples

4 apples
1/2 cup light brown sugar
2 Tablespoons cinnamon

4 marshmallows
Granulated sugar
Butter or margarine

Preheat oven to 400°.   Core the apples and place in a baking pan.   Mix the brown sugar and cinnamon.   Sprinkle granulated sugar in the centers of the apples; then fill with the brown sugar and cinnamon mixture.   Dot the tops with butter.   Pour enough hot water to cover the bottom of the pan.   Bake for 45 minutes or until tender.   Spoon liquid over the apples two or three times during baking.

A few minutes before the apples are done, place a marshmallow on top of each center hole.   Spoon liquid over the apples once again before serving. Cool and eat.

Variation: Omit the marshmallows and top with vanilla ice cream before serving.

Dear Parents,

On _____, our class will share the fairy tale "Snow White and the Seven Dwarfs." The day's lessons and activities will center around this fairy tale. Please read below for ways you can help.

Things to send: _____
_____
_____

Volunteers needed to: _____
_____
_____

Follow-up Activities: Ask your child to share the following songs, games, and other activities related to the fairy tale:

_____
_____
_____

Ask your child the following questions about the fairy tale:

_____
_____
_____

Thank you for your cooperation.

Sincerely,

Name the Seven Dwarfs - Follow-Up Sheet

Examples

Snow White and the Seven Dwarfs Mural

Padded Poison Apples

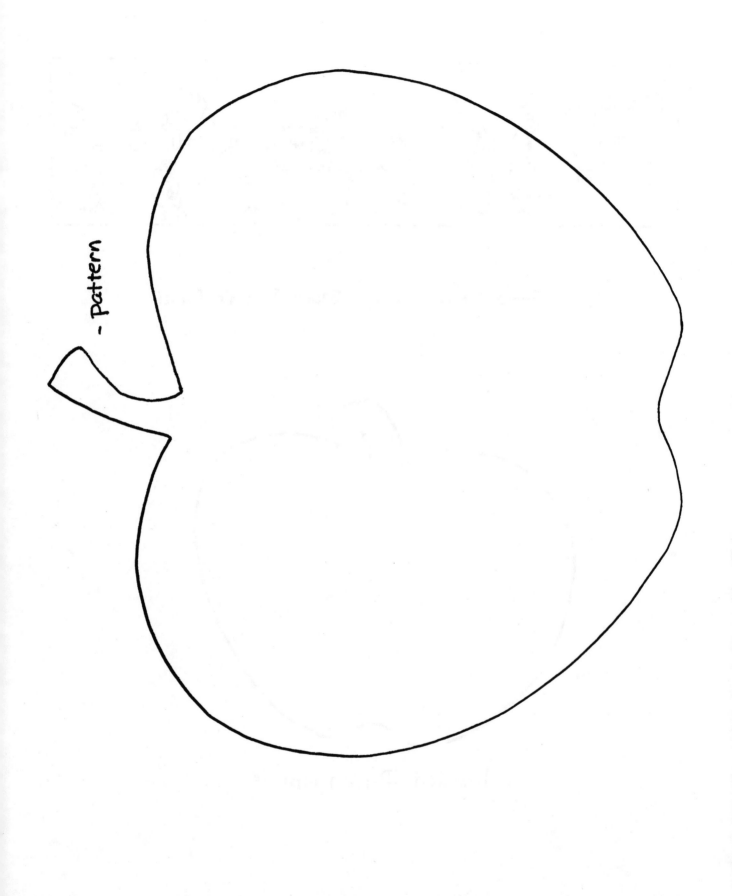

Padded Poison Apples

- pattern

Stick Puppets

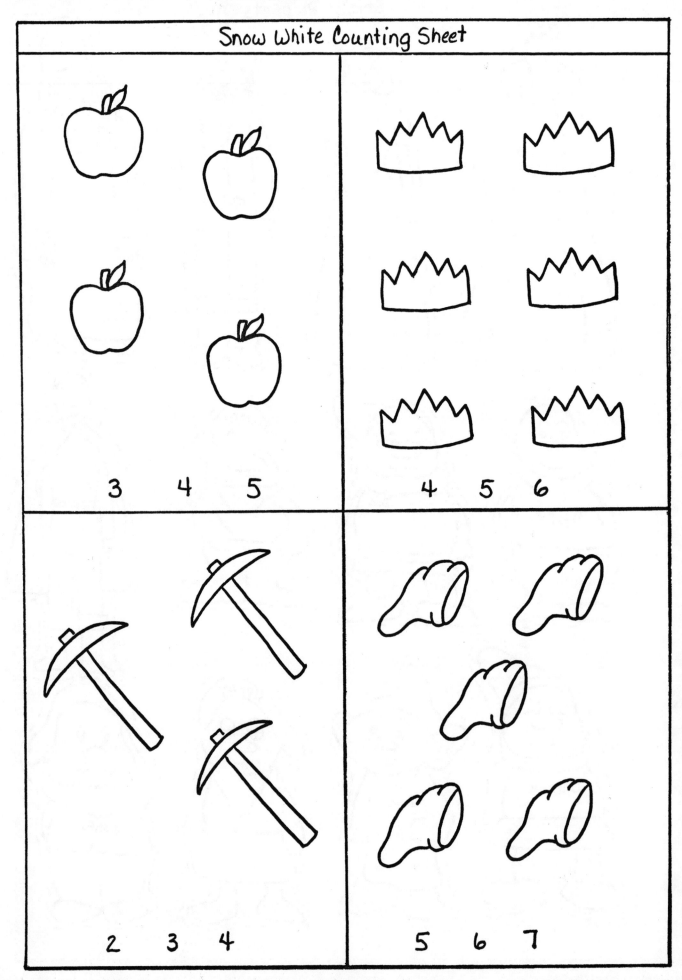

Snow White Counting Sheet

3   4   5

4   5   6

2   3   4

5   6   7

Apple Trees   Name-

1

2

3

4

JACK AND THE BEANSTALK

Source: <u>Jack and the Beanstalk</u> by Tony Ross

LANGUAGE ARTS - SOCIAL STUDIES - SCIENCE

Before the Story

Send home the parents' letter on page 62, if desired. Set out the materials needed for a Live Mural to be made after the story (see example on page 63). You will need a piece of white bulletin board paper long enough to include full-sized pictures of six characters and a beanstalk; tempera paint of various colors; paintbrushes; scissors; a dried bean; and small paper cutouts of a cow, a hen, a bag of gold, and a golden harp. Set aside these materials.

To make a "Story Telling Beanstalk" (see example on page 63), use four double sheets from a newspaper. Beginning at the narrow side of one sheet, roll the sheet into a tube approximately three inches in diameter. Stop rolling a few inches from the end of the sheet, overlap the end of the second sheet and continue. Repeat this procedure until all sheets are rolled into a tube. Mash a little more than one-third of one end of the tube to flatten. Cut into quarters by making four cuts beginning at the end and extending the length of the flattened portion. The cuts should be positioned in the center of each side and on the two folds.

Read the story. When you get to the part about the beanstalk growing, hold the bottom of the "Story Telling Beanstalk" in one hand and pull the cut portions from the other end. Keep pulling until the "beanstalk" is fully extended.

Vocabulary Words

run-down	moldy	bored
prosperous	somber	exquisite
cheated	struggling	hacked
success	bolted	witless
possession	cackles	

After the Story

Set out the bulletin board paper, paints, and paintbrushes. Proceeding from left to right, draw Jack's mother, Jack, the man who gave Jack the bean, the beanstalk, Jack (once again), the giant's housekeeper, and the giant. Draw circles where the heads and arms should be and draw two circles at different heights on the beanstalk. (Use an overhead projector to draw the characters if necessary.) Direct the children to paint the characters and the beanstalk. Cut out the holes.

Select children to hold each side of the mural. Choose other children to be the characters. They should stand behind the mural and put their heads and arms through the holes. The child playing the giant may need to stand on a stool. Jack will move among his two spots and the beanstalk. The giant will also move to the beanstalk when he is chasing Jack. Have one child sit behind the mural and distribute the bean and the paper cutouts to the characters as needed. (The cutouts should be small enough to fit through the holes.)

The remaining children are the audience and sit in front of the mural. After a practice run, read or tell the story while the children act it out. Repeat, using different children for the parts.

Planting Seeds Activity

Pull a plant from the ground and show it to the class. Discuss the parts of the plant and what they do: roots - anchor the plant and collect water and minerals; stem - supports the plant and transports water and food to all parts of the plant; leaves - manufacture food for the plant; flower - makes new seeds.

Display seeds of various sizes and shapes. Help the children identify the seeds. If desired, laminate magazine or workbook pictures of the corresponding fruits, vegetables, etc., and let the children match the seeds and pictures.

Discuss what a plant needs to grow—air, water, sunlight, and food. Then explain and illustrate on the chalkboard the life cycle of a plant seed—planted seed, roots appear, plant pushes above ground, mature plant with stem, leaves, and flowers. To sprout seeds, put moistened paper toweling in a clear plastic cup and place dried beans between the paper toweling and sides of the cup. Keep moist.

Give each child a cup and several dried beans. Set out potting soil and plastic spoons. The children fill the cups with soil and plant the beans. Place in a window and water regularly. When the bean plants are high enough, anchor by tying to popsicle sticks. Let the children make pipe cleaner men to attach to the plants to represent Jack. The bean plants can then be sent home.

Things That Go Together - Sheet

Duplicate and distribute the sheet on page 64. Direct the students to draw lines to match the things that go together, then color the objects.

Choral Poem - "And He Climbed and He Climbed and He Climbed"

Divide the class into eight groups. Teach each group their lines, practice, then perform the choral poem.

Teacher: Jack swapped his cow for a magic bean,
            And grew the tallest beanstalk you've ever seen!

Group 1:   And it grew and it grew and it grew!

Teacher: And Jack said, "I'd like to see the top!"
            So he jumped on the beanstalk and didn't stop.

Group 2:   And he climbed and he climbed and he climbed!

Teacher: Then he reached the top right above a cloud,
            And he heard the giant who was, oh, so loud.

Group 3:   And he hid and he hid and he hid!

Teacher: As the giant ate every single thing in sight,
            Jack swayed and trembled and shook with fright.

Group 4:   And he prayed and he prayed and he prayed!

Teacher: Then the giant fell asleep as giants do,
            And Jack snatched his gold and his singing harp, too.

Group 5:   And he ran and he ran and he ran!

Teacher: As Jack escaped, the harp threw a fit,
            And the giant came after him, lickety-split.

Group 6:   And he raced and he raced and he raced!

Teacher: And Jack, with fear for life and limb,
            Climbed down the beanstalk away from him.

Group 7:   And he climbed and he climbed and he climbed!

Teacher: Then he swung his axe and the stalk did fall,
And down came the giant, meanness and all.

Group 8: And he clapped and he clapped and he clapped!

Teacher: With all that gold, Jack's a millionaire,
But he never eats beans and his mother doesn't care.

All: And he smiles and he smiles and he smiles!

Listening Cans

Collect ten orange juice cans and tops. Rinse clean and dry. Make matching pairs by putting each of the following things in two cans: rice, pennies, jingle bells, dried beans, and dry cereal. Tape the tops closed. Cover with contact paper if desired. The children shake the cans and listen to find the pairs that match.

ART

Jack on the Beanstalk

Preparation - Transfer the pattern on page 65 to a ditto master and duplicate. Cut 8" x 10" pieces of stiff cardboard, 20" pieces of green yarn, and 6" pieces of green crepe paper streamers. Give each child a pattern, a piece of cardboard, a piece of green yarn, and seven pieces of the crepe paper streamers. Provide crayons, scissors, and staplers.

Procedure - Color the pattern of Jack and cut out on the dotted line. Wrap the piece of yarn around the piece of cardboard so that it fits snugly and knot the ends. The yarn should be in the center and extend the length of the cardboard. Tie the crepe paper pieces at intervals on the yarn to represent leaves. Let the teacher staple Jack to the piece of yarn between two "leaves." Gently pull the yarn upward or downward to make Jack climb the beanstalk. (See example on page 65.)

Note: Crepe paper streamers are precut crepe paper on rolls. Regular crepe paper cut into 6" x 1" pieces or green ribbon may be used instead.

"I'm a Giant" Walking Cans

Preparation - Collect two large tin cans of equal size for each child. Turn the cans upside down and make a mark with a permanent marker on either side, an inch or so from the top. Cut two six-foot lengths of heavy string for each child. Provide hammers and large nails.

Procedure - Find the two marks on each can. Punch a hole at each mark with a hammer and nail. To form a handle, thread one piece of string through the holes of one can and tie the ends with a strong knot. Repeat with the other can. Stand on the cans and walk, holding the handles tightly to keep the string stretched. If desired, decorate the cans with stickers or paper cutouts. (See example on page 65.)

Bean Mosaics

Preparation - Purchase different kinds of dried beans. Set out on paper plates. Distribute crayons and glue.

Procedure - Draw an object or scene. Spread an ample amount of glue on a small area and fill in with the beans. Continue in this manner until the object or scene is covered with beans. Dry thoroughly. (See example on page 65.)

Variation: Arrange the beans on the paper to form an object or scene. Pick up one bean at a time, cover one side with glue, and return to the paper.

MATH

Counting Rhyme

Teach the following rhyme:

One, two, the giant's big shoe,
Three, four, the giant slams the door,
Five, six, the giant screams and kicks,
Seven, eight, Jack through the gate,
Nine, ten, with the giant's fat hen.

Measuring Activities

Duplicate the sheet on page 66. Show and explain how to measure with a ruler. Pass out rulers and let the children measure crayons, pencils, and other classroom objects. Distribute the sheets. Direct the children to measure the giant's footprints and Jack's footprints. They should measure from one dot to the other; then write the numbers of inches in the blanks provided.

If you wish to include the measurement of feet in the activity, measure each child and put his or her height on the chalkboard. Compare the different heights. Ask the children to estimate the height of the giant in the story. Measure to the ceiling and record the number of feet on the chalkboard. Compare with the children's estimates of the giant's height.

Spilling the Beans Game

Purchase several packages of dried beans. Draw a large circle on poster paper and cut out. Divide the circle into ten wedges and number the wedges one through ten. Place on the floor with an empty soft drink bottle in the center. Four or five children play the game. Give each player twenty dried beans. The first player spins the bottle. When the bottle stops spinning, the mouth will land on one wedge. The player reads the number on the wedge, then places that many of his or her beans on the floor next to the wedge. The game continues in this manner until one player uses all of his or her beans and shouts, "Spill the beans!" This player wins the game.

Note: The game can be played with more players, but then a longer waiting time is required between turns. This and the number of beans given to each player can be varied according to the children's attention spans.

MUSIC - MOVEMENT - GAMES

Song - "He'll Be Climbin' Down the Beanstalk"

Tune: "She'll Be Comin' Round the Mountain"

He'll be climbin' down the beanstalk when he comes;
He'll be climbin' down the beanstalk when he comes;
He'll be climbin' down the beanstalk,
He'll be climbin' down the beanstalk,
He'll be climbin' down the beanstalk when he comes.

Verses:

   2. He'll be holdin' a fat hen when he comes . . .

   3. He'll be bringin' bags of gold when he comes . . .

4. He'll be with a singin' harp when he comes . . .

5. And the giant will be behind him when he comes . . .

6. He'll be choppin' down the beanstalk when he comes . . .

7. Then we'll count the stacks of gold when he comes . . .

8. And we'll all go out and spend it when he comes . . .

Song - "Fee Fie Fo Fum"

Tune: "Twinkle, Twinkle, Little Star"

Fee Fie Fo Fum (2 beats for first 3 words)
I smell the blood of a little one!
Be he live or be he dead,
I'll grind his bones to make my bread.
Fee Fie Fo Fum
I smell the blood of a little one!

Movement - "On the Beanstalk"

Place a balance (or walking) board on a carpeted area in the classroom. This will be the beanstalk. Have beanbags, plastic hoops, a long rope, and a ball available. Ask the children to remove their shoes and socks unless they are wearing tennis shoes. Stand at one end of the balance board and line up the children at the other end. One by one the children follow the directions below. Teacher directions are in parentheses. Add other activities if desired.

1. Walk forward on the beanstalk keeping your eyes on the teacher.

2. Crawl forward on the beanstalk.

3. Walk backwards on the beanstalk.

4. (Place one beanbag in the center of the balance board.) Walk forward on the beanstalk, step over the beanbag without looking at your feet. (Place two, then three beanbags at intervals on the balance board. Have the children follow the same directions.)

5. Walk forward on the beanstalk with a beanbag on your head.

6. (Place hoops [clouds] on either side of the balance board so that one hoop is diagonal to the other. Provide a rubber ball.) Walk forward on the beanstalk. Stop and bounce the ball one time in each cloud (hoop). Walk to the end of the balance board.

7. Walk forward on the beanstalk, step into each cloud (hoop), walk around the inside of the cloud, then step back on the beanstalk. Repeat with each cloud.

8. Walk forward three steps, then balance on one leg to the count of three. Repeat until you reach the end of the beanstalk.

9. Hop on your left foot to the center of the beanstalk, then hop on your right foot to the end of the beanstalk.

10. (Wrap the rope around and around the balance board leaving spaces in between.) There's a snake on the beanstalk! Walk forward stepping over the snake.

11. Walk forward stepping over the snake without looking at your feet.

12. Hop forward on the spaces formed by the snake.

13. Run forward on the spaces formed by the snake.

14. Stop in each space formed by the snake. Bounce the ball once in the space in front of you. Repeat until you reach the end of the beanstalk.

15. Walk forward stepping on the snake only.

Game - "Jack and the Giant"

Have the players stand in a circle and practice passing a beanbag from hand to hand as quickly as possible around the circle. To play the game, one player holds the beanbag which represents "Jack." Give another beanbag, the "Giant," to a player on the opposite side of the circle. Tell the players that the "Giant" is going to chase "Jack." At the cue, the players pass both beanbags as quickly as possible in the same direction. The fun is in seeing whether the "Giant" catches "Jack," or "Jack" catches the "Giant."

FAIRY TALE KITCHEN

Jack's Beanstalks

1 can refried beans (15 oz.)	Celery stalks
1 1/2 cups sour cream	Cheddar cheese, grated
1/2 teaspoon garlic powder	Tomatoes, chopped fine

For bean dip, combine refried beans, sour cream, and garlic powder. Cover and refrigerate. Rinse and dry celery stalks. Cut into 3" pieces. Stuff with bean dip. Sprinkle on tomatoes and grated cheese.

Dear Parents,

On _____, our class will share the fairy tale "Jack and the Beanstalk." The day's lessons and activities will center around this fairy tale. Please read below for ways you can help.

Things to send: _____

_____

_____

Volunteers needed to: _____

_____

_____

Follow-up Activities: Ask your child to share the following songs, games, and other activities related to the fairy tale:

_____

_____

_____

Ask your child the following questions about the fairy tale:

_____

_____

_____

Thank you for your cooperation.

Sincerely,

Examples

Live Mural

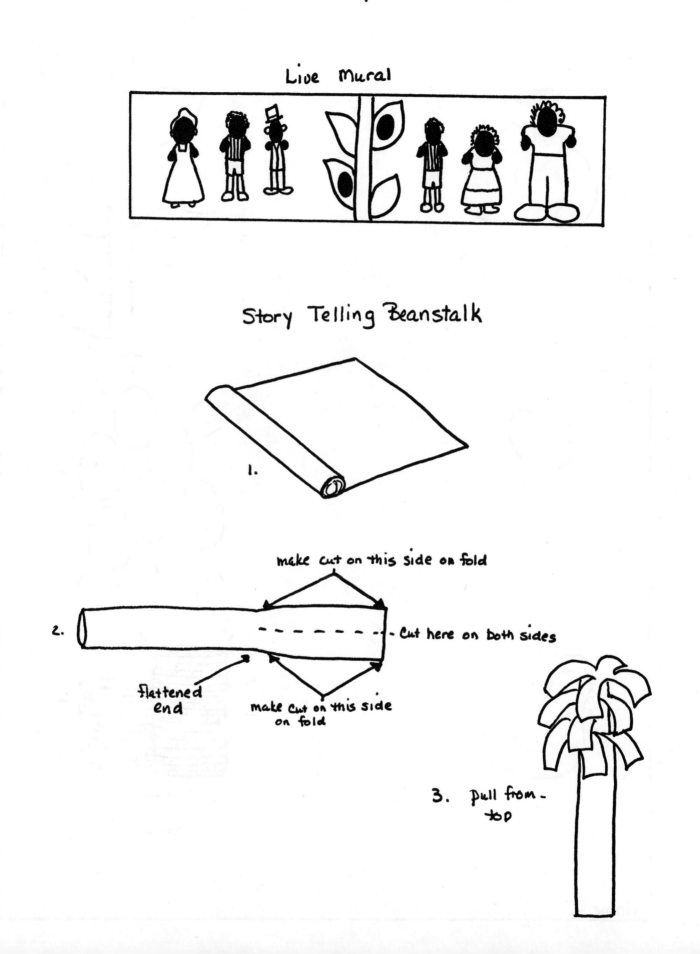

Story Telling Beanstalk

1.

make cut on this side on fold

2. Cut here on both sides

flattened end

make cut on this side on fold

3. pull from top

Things That Go Together

Name -

Examples, Pattern

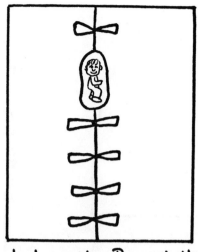

Jack on the Beanstalk
example

Jack on the Beanstalk
pattern

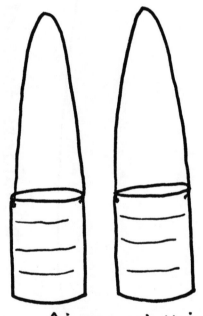

I'm a Giant - Walking
Cans

Bean Mosaics

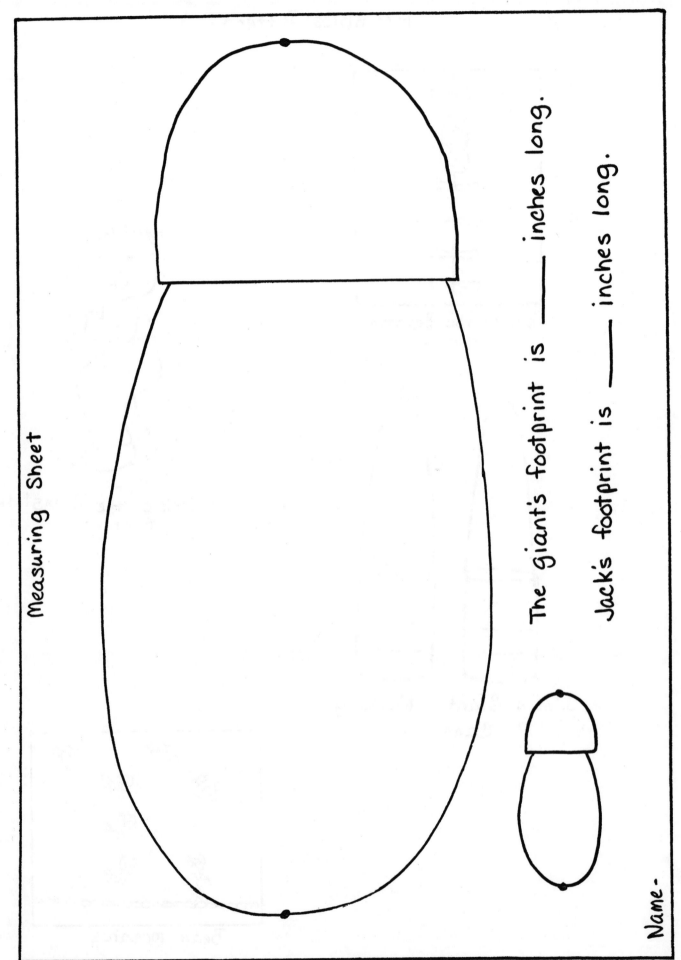

Measuring Sheet

The giant's footprint is ____ inches long.

Jack's footprint is ____ inches long.

Name-

DUMBO OF THE CIRCUS

Source: "Dumbo of the Circus" - <u>Walt Disney's Fantasyland</u>

LANGUAGE ARTS - SOCIAL STUDIES - SCIENCE

Before the Story

Send home the parents' letter on page 76, if desired. Draw a large circus tent on bulletin board paper. Let the children assist in painting the tent. Staple to cover the house side of the Story Area Back Drop (see Room Environment, page 1).

Show a film about the circus or display a picture of a circus in progress. Identify the circus tent, the three rings, the performers, and so forth.

Use pellon to make the flannel board patterns on pages 77 and 78. Color with permanent markers and cut out. Place the flannel board figures and a flannel board on the Display Table. Tell a summarized version of the story, "Dumbo of the Circus," placing the flannel board figures on the flannel board.

Vocabulary Words

winter quarters	compartment	lonesome
ringmaster	messenger	springboard
musicians	receipt	crows
acrobats	freak	cawing
animal trainers	bewildered	applause
trapeze artists	roustabouts	manager
calliope	prison car	
storks	disgrace	

After the Story

Let the children retell the story, placing the flannel board figures on the flannel board. Assist when necessary. Afterwards, ask the following questions:

1. Why did (almost) everyone make fun of Dumbo?
2. If you were Dumbo, how would you feel if people laughed at you?
3. How do you feel about the people and animals who laughed at Dumbo? About Timothy?

4. Has anyone ever made fun of you? Why? How did you feel?
5. Is it bad to be different?
6. Do you have something that makes you self-conscious?
7. What did Timothy teach Dumbo about being different?
8. How do you think the other elephants felt when they saw Dumbo fly? How do you think Dumbo felt? His mother? Timothy?

Alphabet Circus Train

Collect a medium-sized corrugated cardboard box for each child. Cut away the tops and bottoms and write an alphabet letter on the sides of each box. (See example on page 82.) These are the cars of the train. Set in random order on the floor.

Make an Alphabet Picture Necklace to go with each car. Draw a simple circus-related picture, beginning with the letter on the side of the car (for example, an acrobat for the **A** car, a bear for the **B** car, a clown for the **C** car, and so forth.) Punch a hole at the top of each picture and attach yarn to make the necklace. (See example on page 82.) Give each child a necklace; then assist in identifying and discussing the beginning sounds of each.

Tell the children, "This is our Alphabet Circus Train, but the cars are out of order. Which car comes first in the alphabet?" Call on a child to respond and place that car in front. Repeat until the cars are in a line in alphabetical order.

Now tell the children, "The Alphabet Circus Train will be leaving soon, but the cars are empty. What belongs in the **A** car?" The child with the **A** Alphabet Picture Necklace should answer, "I do. I am an acrobat." (Other children may assist if this child doesn't respond.) This child steps inside the **A** car and picks it up, holding it around his or her waist. Repeat with each car. After all cars are filled, shout "All Aboard!", and, if possible, ring a bell. The children imitate a train by holding the boxes and walking in a line behind the first car.

Variation: You may wish to have fewer cars and include only the alphabet letters you are currently teaching. In this case, make several Alphabet Picture Necklaces for each car. Give one to each child and alternate their turns in the cars.

Variation: Leave the bottoms of the boxes intact and put the boxes in alphabetical order on the floor. Collect objects beginning with the letters written on each train car. Mix these and place on the floor. The children place the objects in the proper cars. Examples: **A** car - apple, (toy) ape, (toy) axe; **B** car - banana, bucket, bowl; **C** car - (toy) cat, (toy) car, cup.

Action Story - "Big News"

Assign each of the key words below to a student or group of students. Teach the verbal responses and actions for the key words. After a practice run, read through the story pausing briefly at each key word to let the students stand and perform the responses and actions.

Key Word	Verbal Response	Action
Boy Reporter	"Where's the news?"	Look left and right
circus	"Yeh!"	Outline tent shape in air
fly(ing)	"It's a bird, it's a plane . . ."	Flap arms
elephant(s)	"Doo-doop-de-doo"	Swing arm for trunk
Dumbo	"Hurray for Dumbo!"	Flap hands beside ears
big news	"Extra! Extra!"	Wave imaginary newspaper
monkey	"Eee-eee"	Scratch under arms
pencil and pad	"Scratch-Scratch"	Pretend to write on left hand
Mary Lou	"I'll tell Mommy!"	Thumb in mouth
walk(ing)	"Here we go!"	Walk in place
popcorn	"Pop-Pop"	Jump up and down
run	"Puff-Puff"	Run in place
ringmaster	"Ladies and Gentlemen"	Outstretch arms
mouse	"Squeak-Squeak"	Pretend to jump on chair

Hello out there! Michael Kent, BOY REPORTER here. I just received an inside tip that today, here in our little town, the CIRCUS is arriving! And with this CIRCUS is, get this, an alleged FLYING ELEPHANT named DUMBO. I know. I don't believe it either, but we BOY REPORTERS have to be prepared. No, I think that's the Boy Scouts, isn't it? We BOY REPORTERS have to sniff out the BIG NEWS. Yeah, that's it. So I'm about to check it out. Do you want to come along? Okay, but remember, you're with an official member of the press; so no MONKEY business! Ha! Ha!

First let me put on my BOY REPORTER trench coat, my BOY REPORTER hat, and get my BOY REPORTER PENCIL AND PAD. Oh yeah, and my little sister, MARY LOU—Mom's making me take her, too! Yuk! Now we have to WALK a few blocks, and there's a CIRCUS tent. Boy, is it huge! Let's give the lady our tickets and find a seat. Big crowd here today, folks! Okay, okay, MARY LOU. We're currently WALKING to the POPCORN booth to get some POPCORN for MARY LOU. RUN, MARY LOU, or we'll miss the show. Let me get out my BOY REPORTER PENCIL

AND PAD.   I can't miss a thing.   There's the RINGMASTER and . . . What? Okay, MARY LOU.   Here we go again to the refreshment stand for a cold drink for MARY LOU.   Now we're RUNNING back to our seats. Look, MARY LOU, jugglers, acrobats, and tigers!   Quit crunching that POPCORN so loudly!   The RINGMASTER is announcing the next act, DUMBO, the FLYING ELEPHANT! Hmm, I still don't believe it!   There are the ELEPHANTS WALKING in a line.   The small one at the end must be DUMBO—big ears, red hat, and yes, a MOUSE is standing inside the hat! Now DUMBO, along with the MOUSE, is climbing to the top of a tall house in the center ring.   He's looking out the window.   The drum rolls are deafening! What, MARY LOU! You can't wait! Oh, MONKEY tails! We're now RUNNING to the bathroom.   Hurry up, MARY LOU!   I hear the crowd applauding.   Now I hear them shouting, "He's FLYING!   DUMBO is FLYING!"   Hurry up, MARY LOU!   How can any self-respecting BOY REPORTER get the BIG NEWS when his little sister . . . Oh, there you are.   Come on, let's RUN!   Oh, no, the show is over!

What's a BOY REPORTER to do?   How can I write my story for the newspaper now?   I know—come here, little boy.   Wait, let me get out my BOY REPORTER PENCIL AND PAD.   Now, did you see DUMBO FLY?   You were in the bathroom?   What about you, little girl?   You were at the POPCORN booth?   Pardon me, Lady, did you see DUMBO FLY?   You did? He did? Wow, what a story this will make!   I can see it all in tomorrow's headlines, "BOY REPORTER Sees ELEPHANT FLY."   I'll be famous!   My name will be in lights!   No, MARY LOU, no more POPCORN!   We're going home!   I've got BIG NEWS!

Days of the Week Elephants

Duplicate the sheets on pages 79 and 80.   Draw larger versions of the seven elephants in a line (trunk to tail) on the chalkboard.   With colored chalk, make each elephant a different color and label with the days of the week.   Point to each and read the name of the day.   Then let the children repeat this procedure.   Distribute the sheets.   Direct the children to color and cut out the elephants.   Then the children practice saying the days of the week as they place the elephants in a line in front of them.   You may wish to provide storage envelopes by folding sheets of paper in half and stapling on each side.

Fingerplay - "A Little Gray Elephant"

I've seen silver planes up high   ("Fly" hand over head)

And pretty birds glide in the sky,   ("Fly" other hand over head)

But I'd fall over if I did spy,   (Hand over eyes, look up, sit down)

A little gray elephant flying by.   (Flap hands beside ears)

Dumbo Color Sheet

Duplicate and distribute the sheet on page 81. If necessary, write each color word on the chalkboard and, with colored chalk, make a square of the correct color beside each word. The students color the sheet as indicated.

Things That Fly, Things That Swim

Draw the following things on the chalkboard: a bird, a fish, a butterfly, a snake, a bee, a frog, a dragonfly, a turtle, Dumbo, and a whale. Select different volunteers to circle the things that fly and underline the things that swim.

ART

Dumbo Masks

Preparation - Obtain paper plates and tongue depressors. Cut two holes for eyes in each paper plate. Make cardboard patterns of the elephant ear on page 83. Cut a 2½" x 12" strip of white construction paper per child. Give each child a paper plate, a tongue depressor, a white construction paper strip, and two sheets of white construction paper. Set out crayons, glue, scissors, the cardboard patterns, and scraps of construction paper.

Procedure - Trace the ear pattern on each sheet of white construction paper. Color the ears, the face (paper plate), and the trunk (2½" x 12" strip). Fold the trunk accordion-style, then glue two or three inches below the eyes. Cut out, then glue the ears on either side of the paper plate. Using a generous amount of glue, attach the tongue depressor at the bottom and back of the paper plate. (It will be hidden in front by the elephant's trunk.) Dry well. Draw and cut out a hat from construction paper and glue at the top of the paper plate. (See example on page 82.)

Dumbo Finger Puppets

Preparation - Duplicate the patterns (see page 84) on heavy white construction paper and cut apart. Give each child one pattern. Provide crayons or markers and scissors.

Procedure - Cut out the pattern. Add facial features and color as desired. Bend the pattern at the circle. Make a small cut in the center of the circle. Unbend. Insert one blade of the scissors in the small cut; then cut out the circle to make a hole. Put your finger in the hole to make Dumbo's trunk. (See example on page 82.)

Circus Painting

Preparation - Purchase large white construction paper or cut sheets of white butcher paper. Mix tempera paints of various colors and set out along with paintbrushes. Use a marker to draw a circus ring at the bottom of each sheet. Distribute. Discuss the various acts performed in the three rings of the circus.

Procedure - Paint your favorite circus performer(s) in the circus ring on your paper. (See example on page 82.)

Dumbo the Flying Elephant

Preparation - Duplicate the patterns on page 85. Cut apart and distribute one to each child. Also pass out plastic straws, one per child. Set out crayons, scissors, and staplers.

Procedure - Cut out and color the pattern. Fold the ears backwards and crease on the dotted lines. Repeat, folding the ears forward; then flatten both ears. Turn the elephant over and staple the straw to the back. The top of the straw should be even or below the top of Dumbo's head. Hold the straw in one hand. Wave it back and forth to make Dumbo's ears flap. (See example on page 82.)

MATH

Dumbo's Booklet of Opposites

Write the following words on separate ditto masters: big, small, tall, short, happy, sad, up, down, fat, skinny. Duplicate a set for each child. Assemble and staple at the top. Distribute along with two sheets of construction paper for the covers. Provide crayons or markers. Discuss the words and possible examples of each. The children should draw and color something from the story to represent the word on each page, then decorate the covers. Staple the covers onto the booklets.

Count the Peanuts

Purchase a large bag of unshelled peanuts and place in several bowls. Seat four or five children around each bowl. Give each group a small paper sack containing ten strips of (folded) paper numbered 0-9. The children take turns drawing a number out of the bag, then counting out the correct number of peanuts from the bowl. When there are no more peanuts in the bowl, the players count their peanuts. The player with the most peanuts is the winner for that round. The strips are returned to the bag and the peanuts returned to the bowl for the next round.

Note: If all of the strips have been drawn during a round and there are still peanuts in the bowl, the strips must be put back in the paper sack to complete the round.

MUSIC - MOVEMENT - GAMES

Song - "Dumbo"

Tune: "Bingo"

There was a circus elephant
And Dumbo was his name-O,
D-U-M-B-O,
D-U-M-B-O,
D-U-M-B-O,
And Dumbo was his name-O.

He had two great big floppy ears
That dragged across the floor-O,
D-U-M-B-O,
D-U-M-B-O,
D-U-M-B-O,
And Dumbo was his name-O.

The others laughed until the day
That Dumbo learned to fly-O,
D-U-M-B-O,
D-U-M-B-O,
D-U-M-B-O,
And Dumbo was his name-O.

So remember every big dark cloud

Has got a silver lining,

(Remember) D-U-M-B-O,

(Remember) D-U-M-B-O,

(Remember) D-U-M-B-O,

And Dumbo was his name-O.

Song - "When I See an Elephant Fly" - words by Ned Washington, music by Oliver Wallace

Source: The Greatest Hits of Walt Disney (LP)

Song - "Do Your Ears Hang Low?"

Source: Wee Sing Silly Songs (book and cassette) - Pamela Conn Beall and Susan Hagen Nipp

Movement - "Circus Activities"

Tightrope (Highwire) - Use a balance board or a long strip of masking tape on the floor for the tightrope.   One at a time, the children walk, hop, run, bounce a ball, balance beanbags (on different parts of their bodies), etc., on the "tightrope." If desired, play circus music while the children perform.

Three Rings - Make three rings of masking tape or by placing jump ropes on the floor.   The children perform the following activities in the rings. (Teacher directions are in parentheses.)

1. Horses - walk, trot, gallop around the rings

2. Lions - (Place chairs inside the circles and choose a lion tamer for each ring.)   Lion tamer directs lions to walk on all fours around the ring, jump on chairs, roar, etc.

3. Trick Dogs - (Choose one child in each ring to hold a hoop.)   On all fours, walk, run, sit, lie down, jump through the hoop, etc.

4. Clowns - perform forward and backward rolls, log rolls, stand on head, etc.

Elephant Walk - The children form a circle, bend forward and walk (then run) while swinging one arm to represent the elephant's trunk. Or, play and follow the directions of "The Elephant" from Learning Basic Skills Through Music, Volume I (LP) by Hap Palmer.

Game - "Feeding the Elephants"

Purchase a large bag of peanuts. The children choose partners. Partners are blindfolded and sit side by side at a table. Place an equal number of peanuts in front of each child. At the cue, the children shell the peanuts and feed them to their partners.

Game - "Peanut Drop"

Purchase peanuts. Set a large wide-mouthed jar on the floor. Each player attempts to drop ten peanuts, one at a time, into the jar. The player who drops the most peanuts into the jar wins the game.

Variation: Divide the class into teams and provide a jar for each team. Keep score on the chalkboard.

Game - "Peanut Toss"

Purchase peanuts. Set a coffee can or basket on the floor. Players attempt to toss peanuts into the can or basket. Keep score if desired.

FAIRY TALE KITCHEN

Peanut Butter

1 lb. roasted peanuts
Peanut oil, a few drops
Salt
Crackers

Shell peanuts and place in a blender. Add a few drops of peanut oil. Blend to desired consistency. Salt to taste. Spread on crackers. Yield: 1 cup

Dumbo's Favorite Peanut Butter Candy

1/2 cup peanut butter
1 cup nonfat dry milk
1/2 cup honey

Combine all ingredients and mix well. Place mixture on wax paper and use fingertips to press into a square approximately ¼" thick. Chill. Cut into 1" squares. Yield: approximately 36 pieces

Dear Parents,

On _____, our class will share the fairy tale "Dumbo of the Circus." The day's lessons and activities will center around this fairy tale. Please read below for ways you can help.

Things to send: _____
_____
_____

Volunteers needed to: _____
_____
_____

Follow-up Activities: Ask your child to share the following songs, games, and other activities related to the fairy tale:

_____
_____
_____

Ask your child the following questions about the fairy tale:

_____
_____
_____

Thank you for your cooperation.

Sincerely,

Dumbo Flannel Board Patterns

Dumbo

Timothy Q. Mouse

Dumbo's Clown Costume.

Mrs. Jumbo

Dumbo Flannel Board Patterns

Dumbo woke up and found himself in this tree.

Little boy in crowd - Spanked by Mrs. Jumbo

Crows

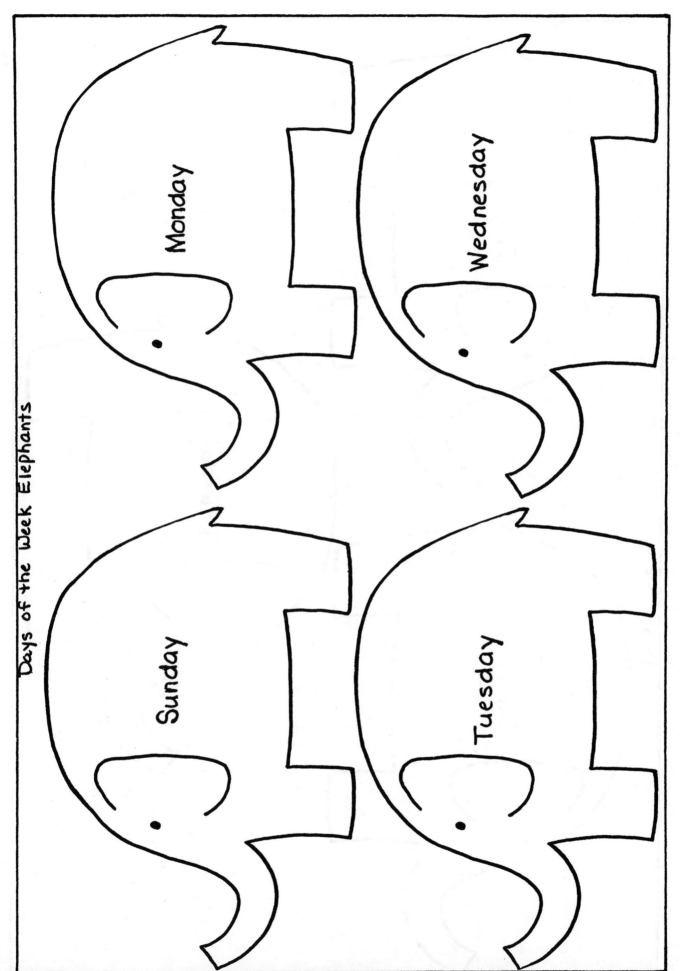

Days of the Week Elephants

Sunday

Monday

Tuesday

Wednesday

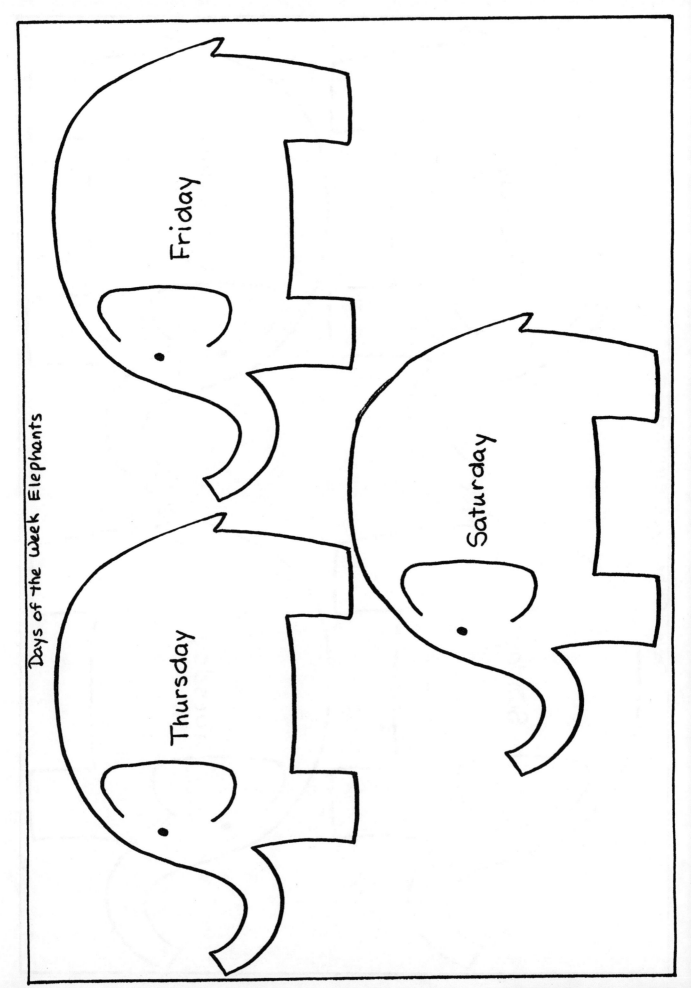

Days of the week Elephants

Friday

Saturday

Thursday

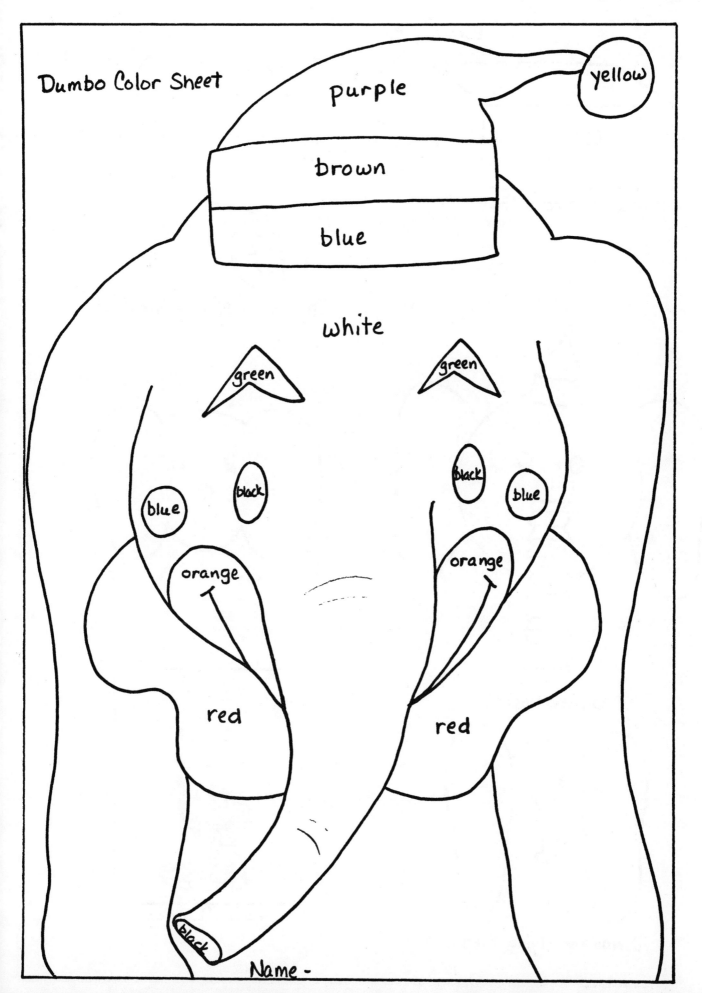

Dumbo Color Sheet

purple

brown

blue

white

green   green

black   black

blue   blue

orange   orange

red   red

black

Name -

Examples

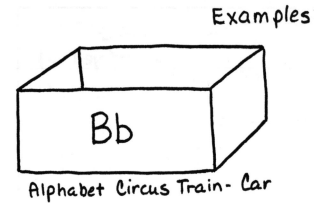

Alphabet Circus Train- Car

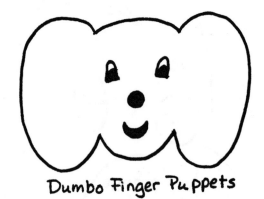

Alphabet Picture Necklace

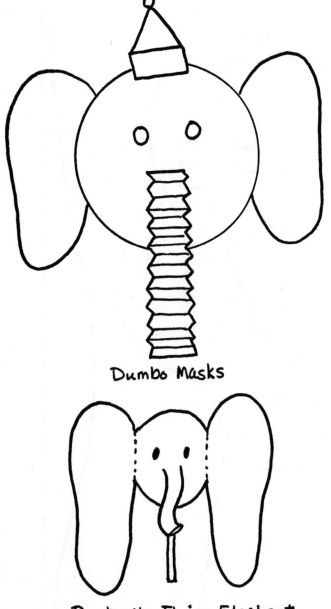

Dumbo Masks

Dumbo the Flying Elephant

Dumbo Finger Puppets

Circus Painting

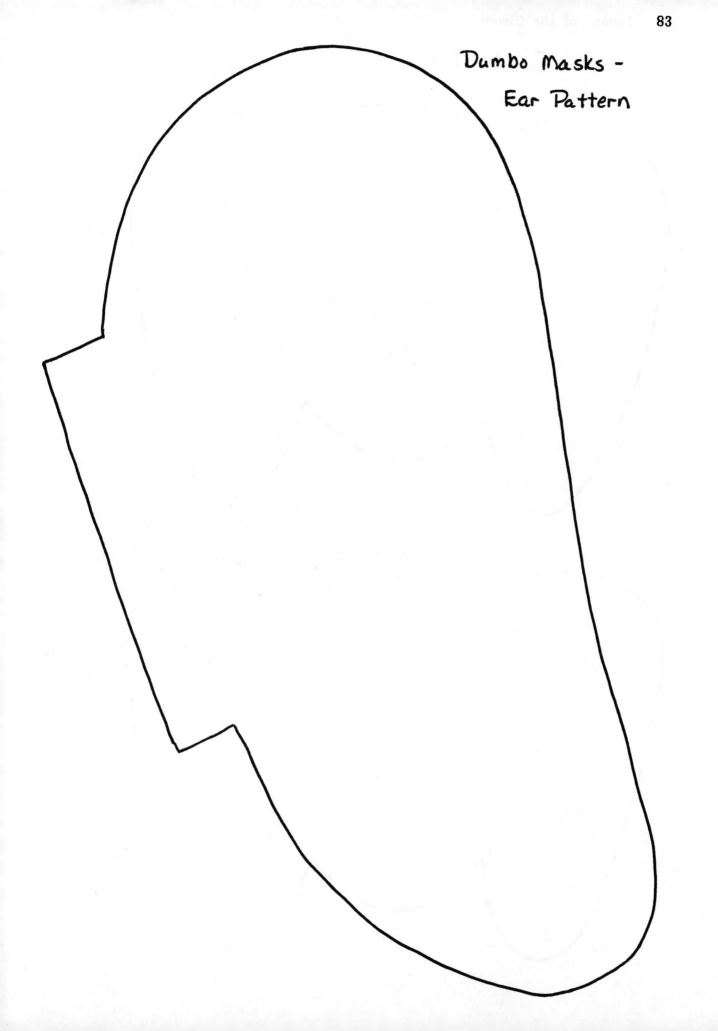

Dumbo Masks -
Ear Pattern

Dumbo Masks -

Dumbo Finger Puppets- Patterns

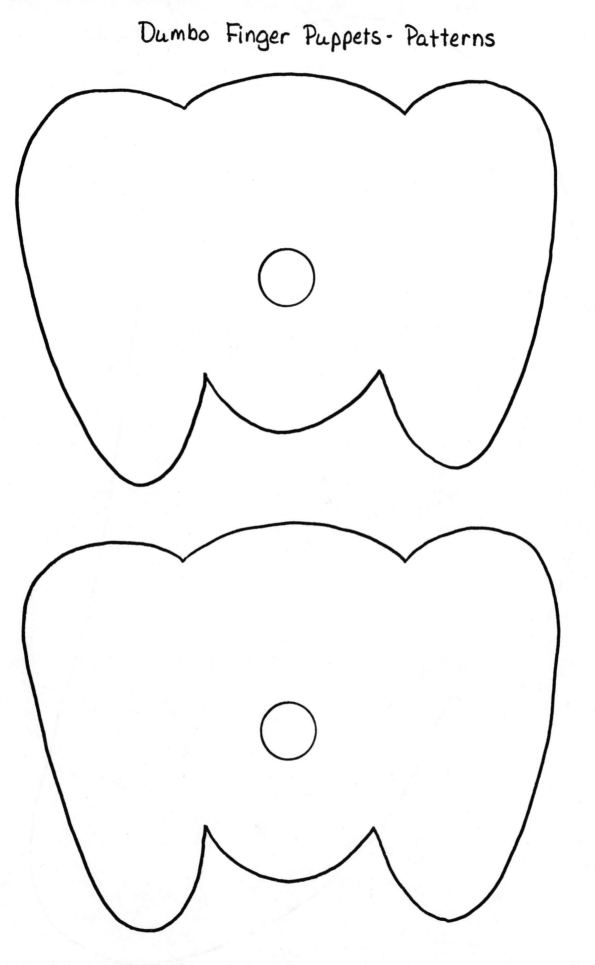

Dumbo the Flying Elephant - Patterns

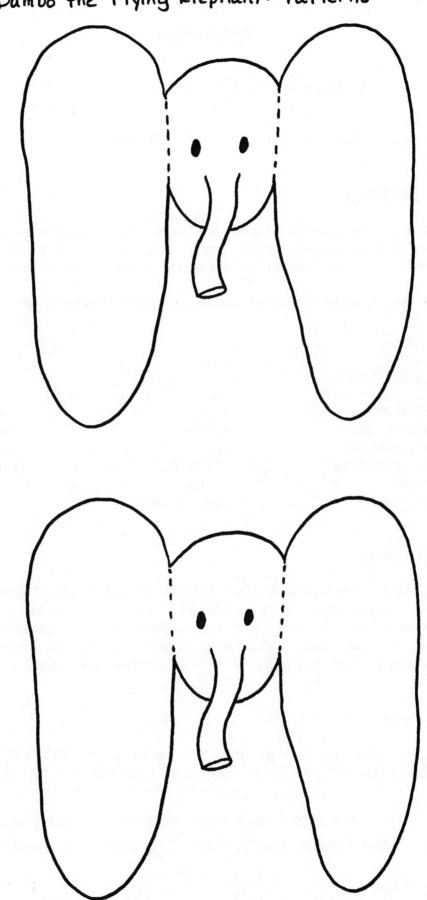

<u>**CINDERELLA**</u>

Source: <u>Walt Disney's Cinderella</u> adapted by Jane Werner

LANGUAGE ARTS - SOCIAL STUDIES - SCIENCE

<u>Before the Story</u>

Send home the parents' letter on page 93, if desired. Display the following items: broom, scrub brush, mop, bucket, a pumpkin, a clock (preferably one that sounds on the hour), a glass (clear plastic) slipper.

Display the following pictures: chickens, geese, horses, cats, dogs, mice, birds.

<u>Vocabulary Words</u>

disrepair	lazy	coachman
stepmother	palace	waltz
stepsisters	ball	midnight
stepdaughter	invitation	servant
cruel	coach	
garret	magic wand	

<u>After the Story</u>

Ask a child to select and identify one of the above display items or pictures and tell what part it played in the story. Repeat with each item and picture. Pass around the items, encouraging the children to discuss how they look and feel. Ask, "What sounds does a clock make?" Hold up each animal picture and ask, "What sound does this animal make?"

<u>Choral Poem</u> - "Me, Oh, My"

Divide the class into four groups. Teach each group their lines and the whole class the last two lines. Practice, then perform the choral poem.

Group 1: The big palace clock began to chime, chime, chime,

And Cinderella said, "Oh! The time, time, time!"

Group 2:   "Me, oh, my, I'd better run, run, run,

              Before this magic spell is done, done, done!"

Group 3:   So down the palace steps she flew, flew, flew,

              Dropping her little glass shoe, shoe, shoe.

Group 4:   "Oh, well," she said, "that's life, life, life!"

              But the Prince said, "Be my wife, wife, wife."

All: So the moral is, never ever contend

              That all good things must come to an end!

Time Activities

Duplicate the sheet on page 94. Using a clock with a second hand, show how time is measured in seconds, minutes, and hours. Explain that clocks tell us what time it is so that we know when to wake up, when to go to school, when to eat lunch, when to go home, and when to go to sleep. Set the clock to indicate the times for each of these activities. Show the time involved in a minute by directing the children to watch the second hand while it makes one complete revolution. Set a kitchen timer for one minute and tell the children, "Raise your hands when you think a minute has passed."

Measure an hour by setting the timer for one hour. Set aside and discuss when the timer sounds. Discuss why time sometimes seems to pass quickly and sometimes seems to pass slowly. Ask the children, "Why did Cinderella forget the time?" Set the clock to indicate midnight and ask, "At midnight, when both hands were on twelve, what happened in the story?" Distribute the sheets. The children draw lines to match the clocks and draw hands on the palace clock as directed. Afterwards, read Clocks and More Clocks by Pat Hutchins.

Character Role-Playing

Secretly assign a character from the story to each child. One child at a time stands before the class saying a few words and acting the part of the character. The other children guess the identity of the character.

Sample Words and Actions:

1. Cinderella - "Thank you, Fairy Godmother!" - smile and look in amazement at dress

2. Stepmother - "Scrub the terrace!" — point finger, look mean

3. Stepsister - "We're going to a ball!" — dance with a smirk on face

4. Stepsister - "My beads!" — grab Cinderella's beads

5. Fairy Godmother - "Bibbidi, bobbidi-boo!" — wave magic wand

6. King - "The Prince must marry!" — pace back and forth in kingly fashion

7. Prince - "May I have this dance?" — bow and extend hand

8. Great Grand Duke - "Of course you may try on the slipper!" — stand straight, use finger and thumb to form monacle

Pumpkins, Pumpkins

Duplicate the sequence cards on page 95. Purchase pumpkins of various shapes and sizes. Let the students examine the pumpkins, noting how they look, feel, and smell. Cut the top from one pumpkin and allow the children to remove the pulp and seeds. Discuss how the pulp and seeds look, feel, and smell. Separate the seeds from the pulp. Discard the pulp and save the seeds for the cooking activity (see Toasted Pumpkin Seeds - Fairy Tale Kitchen). Use the remaining pumpkins in the math activity (see Pumpkin Math - Math).

Place the sequence cards in order on the chalkboard ledge. Refer to the cards as you explain how a pumpkin grows. Shuffle the cards, then place once again on the chalkboard ledge. Call on children to place the cards in sequential order.

ART

Cinderella's Coach

Preparation - Make several cardboard copies of the patterns on page 96 for the children to share. Cut various colors of construction paper in half (6" x 9") and set out along with the patterns, scraps of construction paper, scissors, glue, and crayons.

Procedure - For the coach, trace the pumpkin shape on the half-sheet of construction paper. Trace two circles on scrap paper for the wheels. Glue the wheels at the bottom of the coach. Draw a door on the coach and decorate as desired. (See example on page 97.)

Shapes Mouse

Preparation - Duplicate the sheet (see page 98) on white construction paper. Cut 7" pieces of black yarn. Distribute the sheets and yarn pieces. Provide scissors, glue, crayons or markers, and construction paper scraps. Call on children to identify each shape on the sheet.

Procedure - Cut out the shapes. Glue the bottom point of the triangle marked **X**) near the top of the large circle. Glue the small circles on the remaining points of the triangle. Color. Turn the mouse over and glue the yarn piece at the bottom to form a tail. Draw facial features and clothes on the mouse, or cut these from construction paper scraps and glue on the mouse. (See example on page 97.)

Cinderella's Glass Slipper

Preparation - Duplicate the sheet on page 99 and cut apart for two patterns. Distribute one pattern and a sheet of colored construction paper to each child. Set out silver glitter on paper plates. Provide glue.

Procedure - Cut out the slipper and cover with a generous amount of glue. Sprinkle on glitter. Shake the excess back into the paper plate. Glue the slipper on the construction paper. (See example on page 97.)

MATH

Pumpkin Math

Set the pumpkins (see "Pumpkins, Pumpkins" - Language Arts - Social Studies - Science) on a table. Call on a student to describe one of the pumpkins including its size, shape, color, and unique characteristics. Repeat for each pumpkin. Ask a student to place the pumpkins in order from shortest to tallest. Number each with a permanent marker; then measure. Write each pumpkin's number and height on the chalkboard. Direct the students to determine which pumpkin is the lightest and which is the heaviest. Weigh each on a bathroom scale. List the weights on the chalkboard. Now determine which pumpkin is the thinnest and which is the fattest. Measure with a tape measure. Add the measurements to the list on the chalkboard. Discuss the results.

Seeds in the Pumpkin

Cut the top from one of the pumpkins (above) and remove the seeds. Rinse and dry on paper towels. Duplicate the pumpkin patterns (see page 100) on orange construction paper. Write a different number in the middle of each pumpkin. Set out pumpkin seeds and glue. The children tear the pumpkins on the solid lines, read the numbers in the center, and glue that many seeds on the pumpkins.

Pairs Sheet

Duplicate the sheet on page 101. Explain that a pair is a set of two things that go together; for example, a pair of glass slippers. Ask the students to think of other pairs (socks, mittens, eyes, gloves). Then ask, "Why do we say a pair of scissors and a pair of pants?" (They have two parts which are used together.) Distribute the sheet. The students draw lines to match the pairs, then color the objects.

MUSIC - MOVEMENT - GAMES

Song - "Cinderella"

Tune: "Yankee Doodle"

Cinderella worked all day
To please her mean stepmother,
But every time she did a chore
She heard "Now here's another!"
Cinderella kept it up,
Finished what she started,
Did her best without a rest,
Yes, she was quite stout-hearted.

Cinderella met the Prince
Who was quite sad and lonely,
Soon as he laid eyes on her
He said, "My one and only!"
Cinderella danced all night,
'Til she heard the clock chime,
Being fleet upon her feet,
She was out of there in no time.

Cinderella went back home,

She didn't rush or hurry,

With a fairy godmother for a friend,

You shouldn't have to worry.

Cinderella wed the Prince,

Used the things life taught her,

She was kind to her three maids,

The stepmother and her daughters!

Song - "Bibbidi-Bobbidi-Boo" - by Mack David, Al Hoffman, and Jerry Livingston

Source - <u>The Greatest Hits of Walt Disney</u> (LP)

Game - "Dance With the Ugly Stepsister

Cut off the bottom of a lunch-sized paper bag. Draw the stepsister's face on one side. Slip the bag over the end of a mop so that the mop forms the stepsister's hair. Secure the bag to the mop with a rubber band. An uneven number of players is necessary for the game. Play "Eeny-Meeny-Miney-Mo" to choose the first dance partner for the "Ugly Stepsister." Start the music. The partners dance until the music stops; then they must find another partner. At this time, the player with the "Ugly Stepsister" lays the mop on the floor and joins in. The player without a partner dances with the "Ugly Stepsister." Repeat.

Game - "Clock Search"

Wind an alarm clock and set it to go off in about five minutes. Direct the children to cover their eyes as you hide the clock in the room. Explain the game to the children. When the alarm sounds, the children try to find the clock before the ringing stops. The child who finds the clock hides it for the next round. If the clock isn't found in time, retrieve it, and repeat the procedure.

Variation: Substitute a kitchen timer for the clock.

FAIRY TALE KITCHEN

Toasted Pumpkin Seeds

Rinse the seeds (see "Pumpkins, Pumpkins" - Language Arts - Social Studies - Science) and dry on paper towels. Coat the bottom of a shallow baking pan with cooking oil. Cover the bottom of the pan with a single layer of seeds. Bake at 350° for 20-25 minutes or until golden brown. Stir occasionally. Sprinkle with salt, if desired.

Note: Pumpkins used in the day's activities can be used to make your favorite pumpkin pie or pumpkin bread recipe. Cut the pumpkins into fourths and remove seeds and stringy portions. Cut into smaller pieces, pare, and boil in a small amount of water for 25-30 minutes or until tender. Drain and purée in blender. Use in recipe.

Mouse Cookies

1/2 cup butter or margarine
1 cup all-purpose flour
2 cups sharp Cheddar cheese, grated
1 teaspoon salt
Red pepper, to taste

Mix ingredients together with a spoon; then use hands to blend. Divide dough in half and make two long rolls, approximately 1" thick. Wrap in wax paper and chill. Slice very thin and place on ungreased cookie sheet. Bake at 325° for 10-12 minutes or until light brown. Yield: approximately 100 cookies

Dear Parents,

On _____, our class will share the fairy tale "Cinderella." The day's lessons and activities will center around this fairy tale. Please read below for ways you can help.

Things to send: _____
_____
_____

Volunteers needed to: _____
_____
_____

Follow-up Activities: Ask your child to share the following songs, games, and other activities related to the fairy tale:

_____
_____
_____

Ask your child the following questions about the fairy tale:

_____
_____
_____

Thank you for your cooperation.

Sincerely,

Name:

Time Sheet

Draw a line between the two clocks that match. Draw the hands to read midnight on the Palace clock below.

Palace Clock

Sequence of
a Pumpkin's
Growth -
Cards

seeds

Plant

blossoms

Pumpkins

ripe Pumpkin

Cinderella's Coach · Patterns

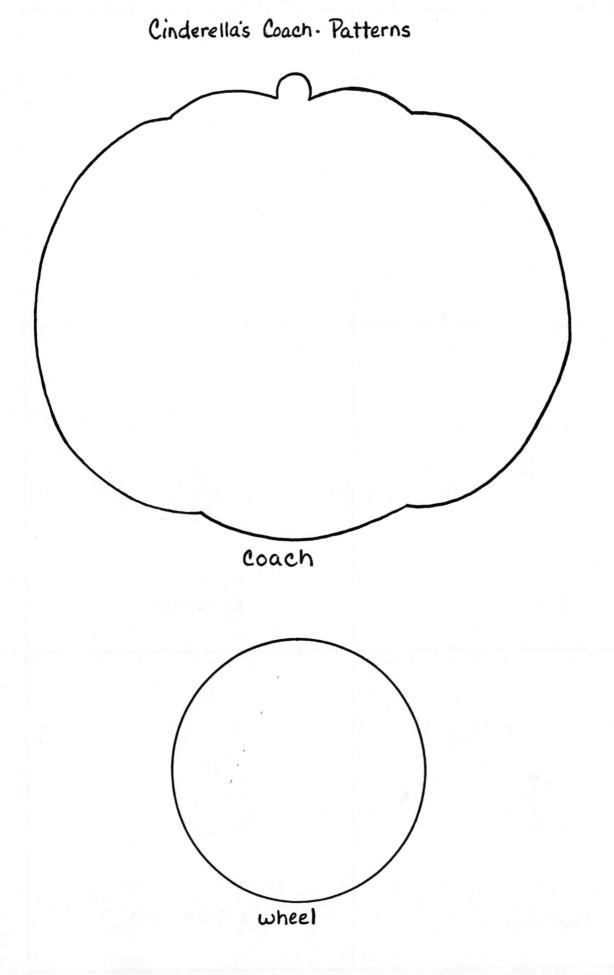

Coach

wheel

Examples

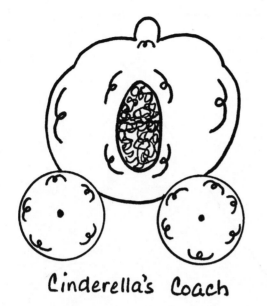

Cinderella's Coach

Shapes Mouse

Cinderella's Glass Slipper

Shapes Mouse

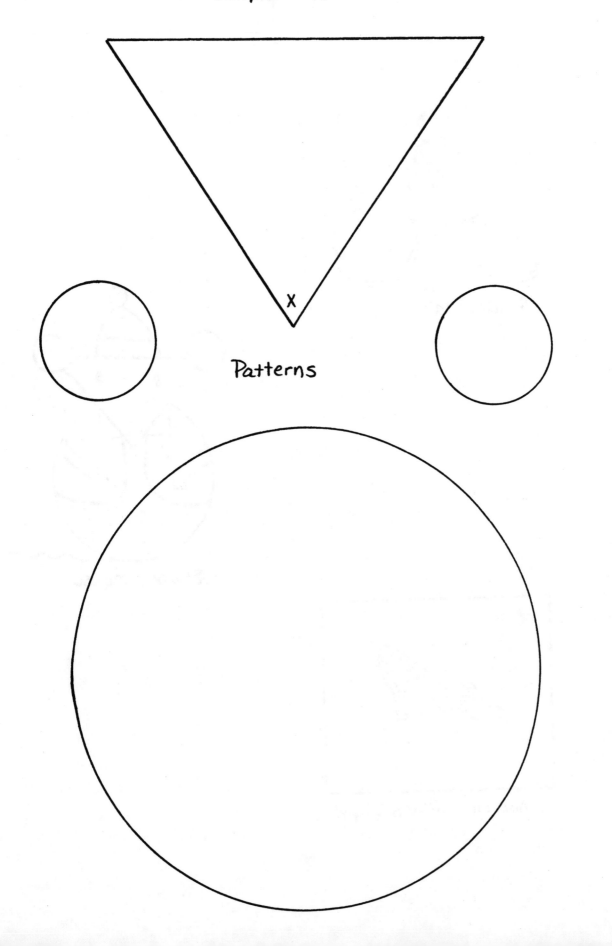

Patterns

X

Cinderella's Glass Slipper - Patterns

Seeds in the Pumpkin · Pattern

Pairs Sheet

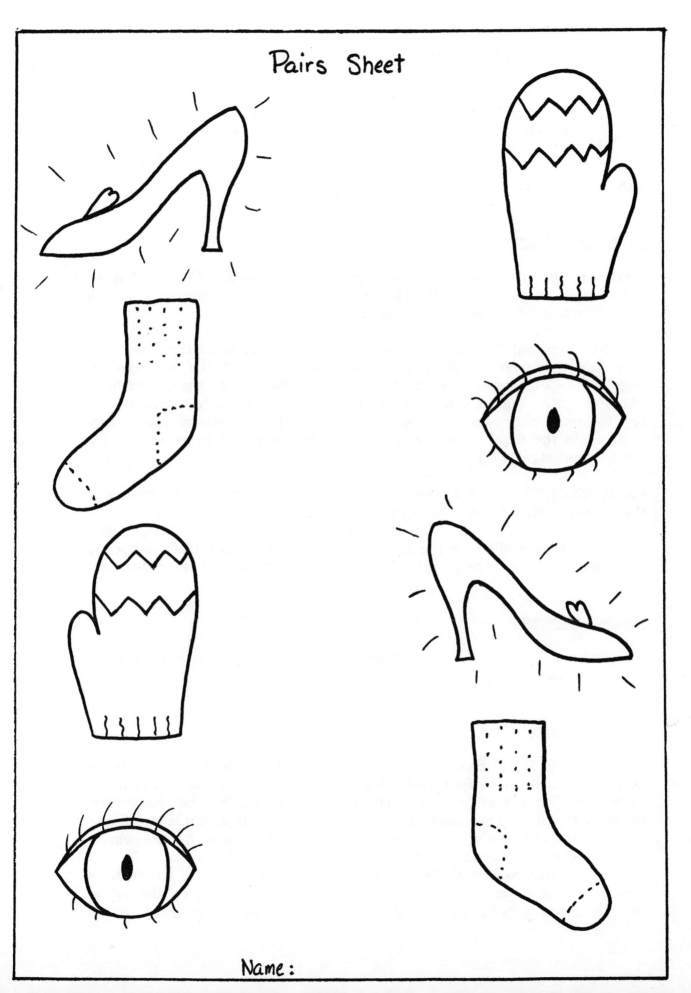

Name:

GOLDILOCKS AND THE THREE BEARS

Source: "Goldilocks," My Big Book of Fairy Tales by Marshall Cavendish Limited, published by Exeter Books

LANGUAGE ARTS - SOCIAL STUDIES - SCIENCE

Before the Story

Send home the parents' letter on page 108, if desired. On the Display Table, place an assortment of bears (stuffed, ceramic, wooden, etc.), and reference and story books about bears.

For the "Chin Skit" to be presented after the story, make three pairs of ears for the bears. Duplicate, color, and cut out the patterns on page 109. Cut four 30" pieces of yarn. Fold the ears on the dotted lines "A" and "B". Unfold and apply a line of glue on each "A" dotted line. Lay the yarn pieces on the glued ("A") lines of each pair of ears. Dry well. Fold the flaps upward and staple to the ears. Trim excess. (See example on page 109.)

For Goldilocks' bow, tie a wide piece of hair ribbon around the middle of the fourth yarn piece and tie into a bow.

Other materials needed for the skit are four scarves or kerchiefs, a spoon, cold cream, an eyebrow pencil, and lipstick. Set aside these materials.

Vocabulary Words

peered	thatched	comfortable
cottage	porridge	prowl

After the Story

For the "Chin Skit," choose four children to play Goldilocks and the three bears. Place three or four tables side by side. Ask the players to lie on their backs on the tables. The children's chins will be the characters' heads in the skit. (See examples on page 109.) Apply a thin layer of cold cream to the children's chins; then draw eyes and noses with the eyebrow pencil. Use the lipstick to color Goldilocks' lips and cheeks. Tie the yarn ears, the bow, and the scarves (or kerchiefs) on the children as shown. To perform the skit, the children lie side by side on the tables with their heads hanging slightly off the ends. Place the spoon beside

Goldilocks. Narrate the story, stopping to let the characters recite the well-known lines. Ifnecessary, insert cues to let the children know when and what to recite. They may also gesture with their hands and move their heads at appropriate times in the story. Goldilocks uses the spoon when she tastes the porridge. If time allows, let other children perform the skit.

Rooms in the House Activity

Obtain three shallow corrugated cardboard boxes and label with tags which read "Kitchen," "Living Room," and "Bedroom." Beside the words, draw a sink, a couch, and a bed. Collect things which are associated with each room (see examples below) and place in front of the boxes on a table. Discuss the setting of Goldilocks and the Three Bears. Ask the students to recall in which room the different scenes occurred. Identify the various items. Direct the students to place the items in the proper "rooms."

Examples: Kitchen - measuring spoons, small pot, potholder, plastic plate and utensils, (empty) dishwashing liquid bottle, roll of paper towels

Living Room - dollhouse furniture (couch, chair), TV Guide, remote control, decorative items

Bedroom - pillowcase, alarm clock, pajamas, slippers, stuffed toy, nightlight

Hard and Soft Sheet

Obtain chips of wood from a lumber company or construction site. Purchase cotton balls. Duplicate and distribute the sheet on page 110. Provide glue. Discuss hard and soft and where these terms were used in the story. Give each child a chip of wood and several cotton balls. Discuss which is hard and which is soft. Direct the children to glue the items on the proper sections of the sheet using an ample amount of glue. Dry thoroughly.

Clapping Rhyme - "Pease-Porridge Hot" - Mother Goose

Teach the rhyme; then have the children choose partners and sit facing each other on the floor. The children recite the rhyme while performing the clapping sequence as follows: partners hold up their hands and clap each other's hands for the first beat, clap their own hands together for the second beat, clap their own thighs for the third beat, then clap their own hands together once again. This sequence is repeated throughout the rhyme.

Pease-porridge hot,

Pease-porridge cold,

Pease-porridge in the pot

Nine days old.

Some like it hot,

Some like it cold,

Some like it in the pot

Nine days old.

Daddy likes it hot,

Mama likes it cold,

I like it in the pot

Nine days old.

What's Missing

Seat the children on the floor in a circle. Ask them to close their eyes.
In the middle of the circle, place a variety of items such as a spoon, a
comb, an eraser, a paper clip, etc. If possible, include three chairs and
three beds from a dollhouse, and three small bowls. Cover the items with
a towel. Ask the children to open their eyes. Uncover the items, let the
children observe them for a few minutes, then have them close their eyes
again. Remove one item. When the children open their eyes, call on a
child to identify what is missing. Return the missing item to the group
and repeat the activity.

Fingerplay - "Goldilocks and the Three Bears"

This is Papa Bear and this is Mama Bear (Raise middle finger, then
pointer finger of right hand)

And this is their tiny Baby Bear (Raise thumb of right hand)

And here asleep is Goldilocks with her curly golden hair. (Hold thumb
of left hand in a horizontal position)

When the bears returned from a walk one day, ("Walk" 3 fingers of right
hand towards left hand)

Goldilocks screamed and ran away. (Raise thumb of left hand quickly and
make it run away)

ART

Fingerpainted Bears

Preparation - Enlarge the bear on page 111 to make a 12" cardboard pattern. On butcher paper, trace one bear for each child. Cut apart. Set out fingerpaints and scissors. Have a spray bottle of water available.

Procedure - Cut out the bear and spray lightly with water. Fingerpaint the bear as desired. Dry.

Goldilocks and the Three Bears Peep Boxes

Preparation - Collect a shoebox for each child. Cut a "window" in the top of each box an inch or two from one end. Cut a peephole in one end of each box. (See example on page 112.) Duplicate and distribute the patterns on page 112. Provide crayons or markers, scissors, and glue.

Procedure - Color the patterns and cut out. Fold back on the dotted lines and spread glue on the tabs (below the dotted lines). Glue the figures inside the box so that they are visible through the peephole. Some of the patterns can be glued to the back "wall" of the box. Cut away the tabs on these patterns. Put the top on the box with the "window" towards the back. Look through the peephole.

MATH

Bear Counting Booklet

Duplicate the booklet covers (see pages 113 and 114) on white construction paper and the booklet pages (see pages 115 through 119) on white unlined paper. Distribute along with scissors and crayons. Direct the students to cut out the covers and pages. Assemble and staple together at the top. Read the sentence on each page. The students color the numbers and objects on each page, then color the covers as desired.

Big/Middle-Sized/Small Math Sheet

Duplicate and distribute the sheet on page 120. Direct the children to circle the big object, underline the middle-sized object, and put an **X** on the small object in each block.

MUSIC - MOVEMENT - GAMES

Song - "Little Cottage in the Wood"

Tune: "Little Cabin in the Wood"

Little cottage in the wood,
Little girl by the window stood,
Three brown bears came walking home,
Walking in the door.

"Help! Help! Help!" yelled Goldilocks,
"Go away, I'm scared of bears!"
"Growl, growl, growl," replied the bears,
And Goldilocks ran home.

Song - "The Bear Went Over the Mountain"

Sources: Disney's Children's Favorites, Volume II (LP)
Wee Sing Silly Songs (book and cassette) - Pamela Conn Beall
and Susan Hagen Nipp

Game - "Porridge Eating Contest"

Collect "TV dinner" aluminum containers, preferably the smaller ones which
have two sections. You will need one for every two children. Cook
enough oatmeal or cream of wheat to provide a helping for each child.
The children choose partners for the contest. Each couple sits side by
side at a table and is provided with two spoons tied together with an
8" piece of string and a "TV dinner" container holding two helpings of
"porridge." At the signal, the contestants use the tied spoons to eat the
"porridge" as quickly as possible. The couple finishing first wins the
contest. Suggested prizes: two copies of Goldilocks and the Three Bears.

Game - "Goldilocks and the Three Bears"

This game is a variation of "Cat and Rat." The players form a circle and
join hands. One player is chosen to be "Goldilocks" and stands inside the
circle. Another player is chosen to be the "Bear" and stands outside the
circle. To begin the game, the "Bear" growls and "Goldilocks" says, "Help!
Help!" Then the "Bear" tries to catch "Goldilocks" by breaking through

the circle. The players help her by raising and lowering their arms to prevent the "Bear" from entering the circle. If the "Bear" is able to enter the circle, any two players may drop their hands and let "Goldilocks" leave the circle. These two players then become the "Door." The "Bear" must also exit through the "Door" to chase "Goldilocks." If Goldilocks makes it around the circle and back through the "Door," she is safe and gets to be "Goldilocks" again for the next round. If "Goldilocks" is tagged, the "Bear" becomes the new "Goldilocks." In either case, a new "Bear" is chosen and the game begins again.

FAIRY TALE KITCHEN

Porridge and Fruit

(Single Serving Recipe)

1 cup cooked oatmeal
1 apple (or pear), chopped
1/2 teaspoon cinnamon
Butter, one pat
Milk
Sugar

After cooking the oatmeal, add the chopped apple (or pear) and cinnamon. Cook for ten minutes over low heat. Place a pat of butter in a bowl. Pour the oatmeal into the bowl. Add a small amount of milk and sugar to taste. Stir and eat when cooled.

Note: This will make one serving or two "taster's portions." Styrofoam coffee cups may be substituted for the bowls.

Dear Parents,

On _____, our class will share the fairy tale "Goldilocks and the Three Bears." The day's lessons and activities will center around this fairy tale. Please read below for ways you can help.

Things to send: _____

_____

_____

Volunteers needed to: _____

_____

_____

Follow-up Activities: Ask your child to share the following songs, games, and other activities related to the fairy tale:

_____

_____

_____

Ask your child the following questions about the fairy tale:

_____

_____

_____

Thank you for your cooperation.

Sincerely,

Chin Skit - Examples, Patterns

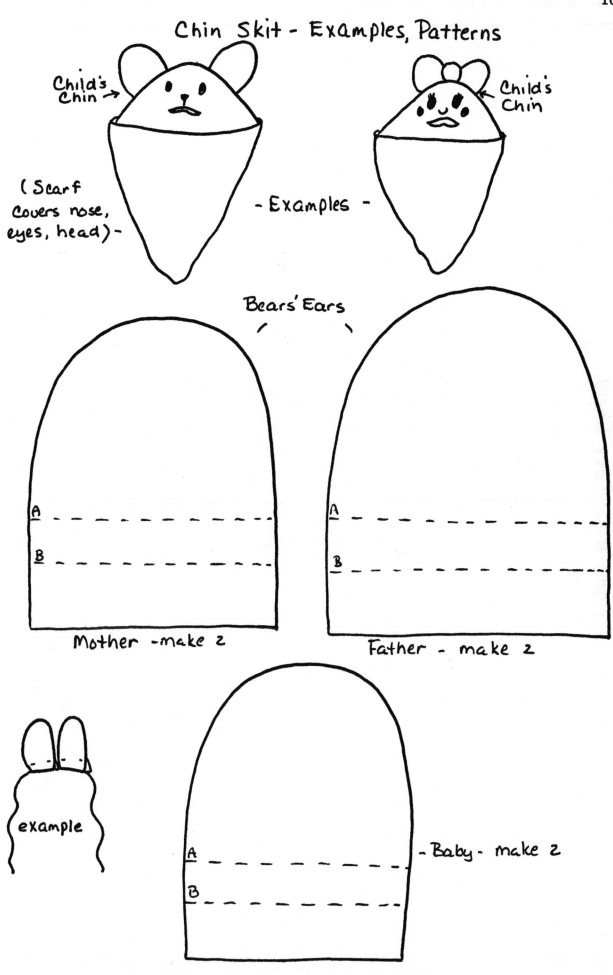

Child's Chin →

Childs Chin ←

(Scarf covers nose, eyes, head) -

- Examples -

Bears' Ears

A
B

Mother -make 2

A
B

Father - make 2

example

A
B

- Baby- make 2

Hard and Soft Sheet

Soft

Hard

Fingerpainted
Bears

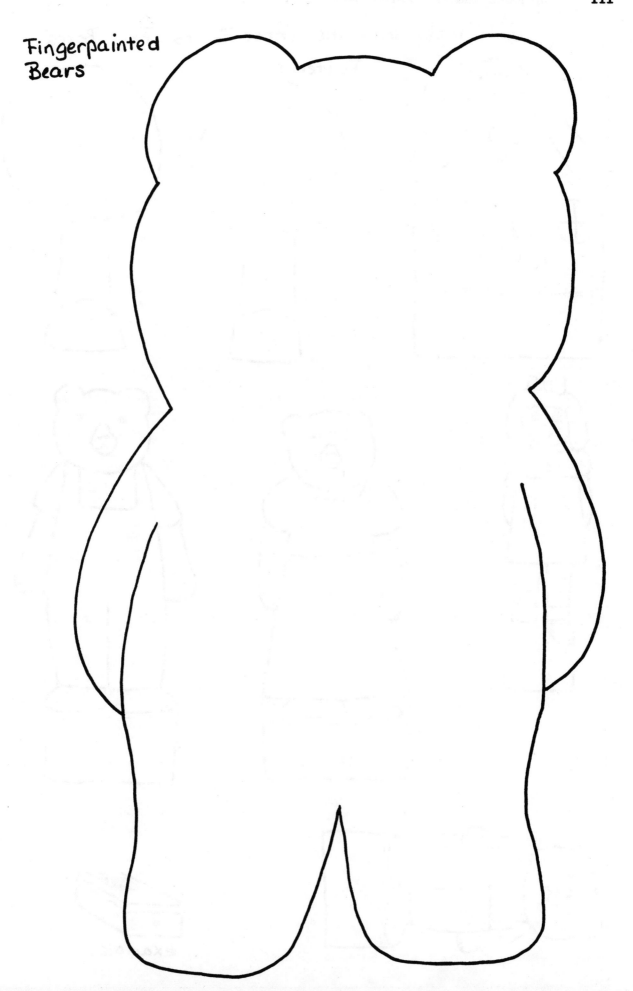

Goldilocks and the Three Bears - Peep Boxes Patterns

example

Front Cover

Bear
Counting
Booklet

Name _____

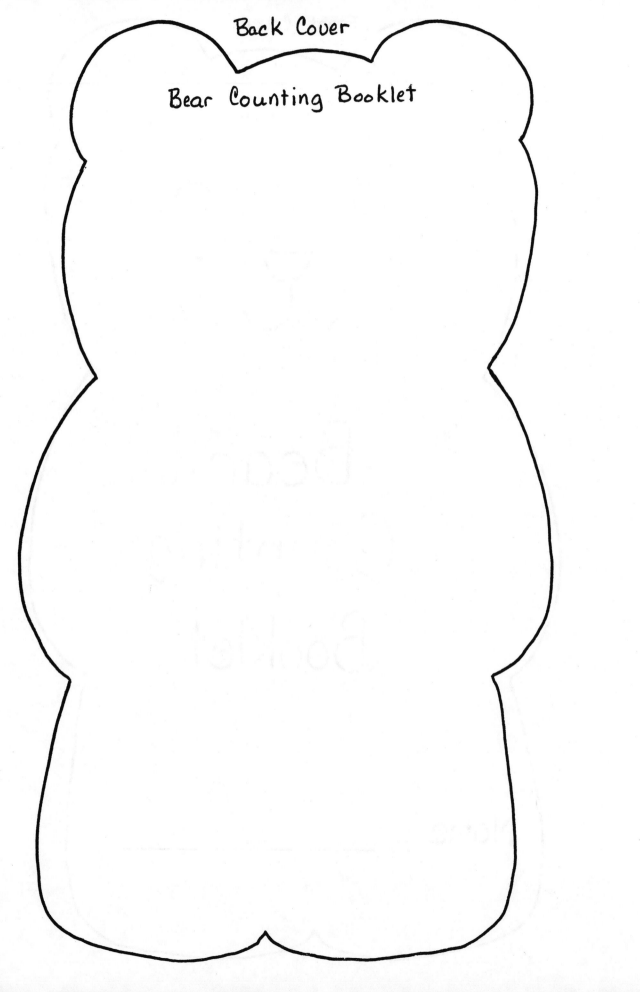

Back Cover

Bear Counting Booklet

Back Cover

Bear Counting Booklet - Pages

The bear has 1 cap.

Bear Counting Booklet- Pages

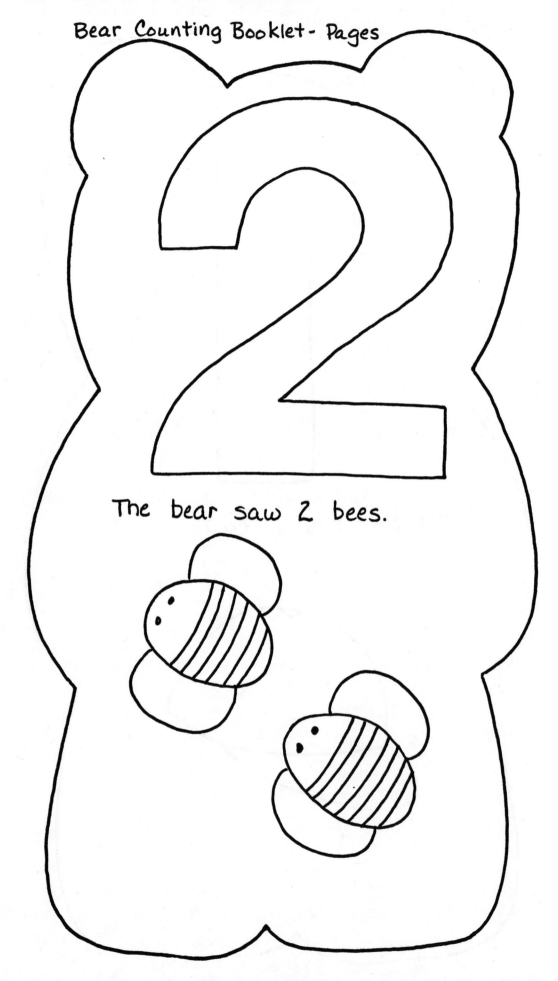

The bear saw 2 bees.

Bear Counting Booklet - Pages

The bear picked 3 flowers.

Bear Counting Booklet· Pages

The bear stacked 4 blocks.

Bear Counting Booklet - Pages

5

The bear bought 5 ice cream cones.

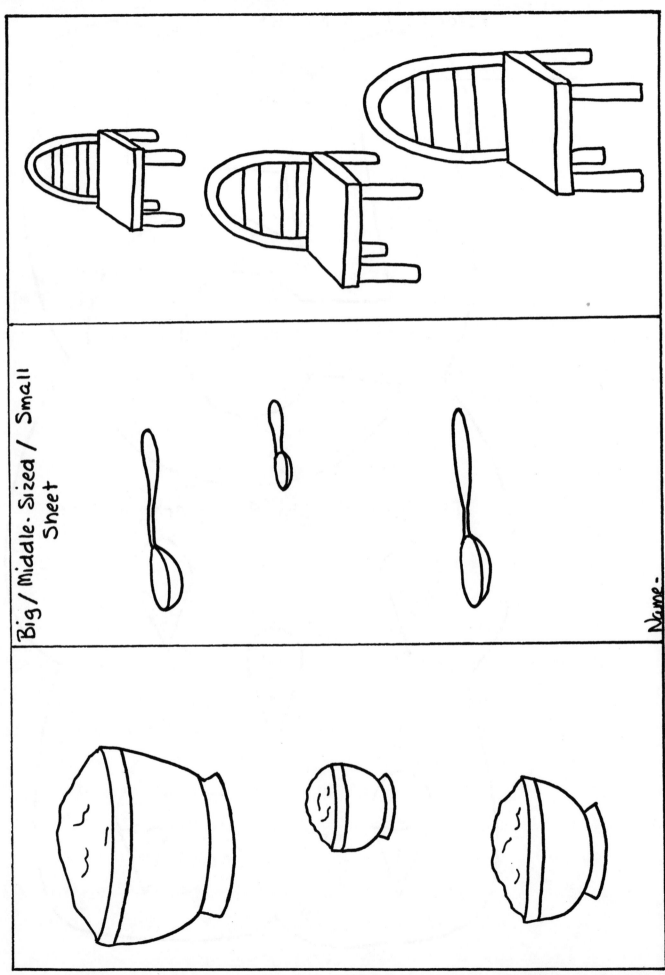

Big / Middle-Sized / Small Sheet

Name.

PETER PAN

Source: <u>Walt Disney's Peter Pan</u>

LANGUAGE ARTS - SOCIAL STUDIES - SCIENCE

Before the Story

A few days in advance, send home the parents' letter regarding "Happy Headgear Day" (see page 129). Send home the parents' letter on page 128, if desired. Using a tape recorder, make a "dialogue" tape of each character in the story. Disguise your voice and/or recruit friends and older students to supply the different "voices." Suggested dialogue for each character:

1. Wendy - "Tonight I will tell you another story of Peter Pan and Never Land."
2. Michael - "John, be quiet. Wendy's telling a story."
3. John - "Where is my teddy bear?"
4. Nana - "Ruff-ruff-time for bed, children!"
5. Peter Pan - "Come with me to Never Land."
6. Tinker Bell - (Tape a bell ringing.)
7. Lost Boys - "Hurray! We got the Wendy bird!"
8. Indians - (Tape Indian war cries.)
9. Tiger Lily - "Thank you, Peter Pan, for saving me, Chief's daughter, from evil Captain Hook."
10. Captain Hook - "Blast it! We still don't have Pan!"
11. Crocodile - (Tape clock ticking.)

Vocabulary Words

nursemaid	mermaid	squaws
duel	jealous	scheming
arch-enemy	toadstool	homesick
nursery	tunnel	walking the plank
pixie dust	disguised	

After the Story

Play the tape, stopping after each character's dialogue. Select volunteers to identify the characters. Afterwards, ask the children to name their favorite character from the story and explain why they like this character more than the others.

Happy Headgear Day

Make a wall or bulletin board display of the various headgear in the story of Peter Pan. Enlarge the patterns on pages 130 and 131 to make Peter Pan's cap, Wendy's bow, Nana's cap, Michael's top hat, the Lost Boys' animal hats, Captain Hook's hat, Indian headdress, Smee's cap, and a pirate's bandanna cap. Assist the students in identifying the headgear and the characters that wear them in the story. Let each student share his or her headgear (see parents' letter on page 129). Put all of the headgear in a row and encourage the students to note and compare the different colors, shapes, sizes, and distinguishing characteristics. Other correlating activities are as follows:

1. Book - Read Caps For Sale by Esphyr Slobodkina. Dramatize the story with the children playing the parts of the peddler and the monkeys.

2. Following Directions Activity - The children hold their headgear, spread out in an open area, and follow the sample directions below.

    a. Hold your headgear in front of you.
    b. Put your headgear on your head.
    c. Put your headgear on the floor in front of you.
    d. Walk in a circle around your headgear.
    e. Pick up your headgear with your right hand.
    f. Put your headgear in your left hand.
    g. Hold your headgear over your head.

3. Rhyming words - On the chalkboard, draw a large top hat, a large cap, and a large bow. Label "hat," "cap," and "bow." Brainstorm for words that rhyme with hat. Write the children's responses on the hat. Repeat with the cap and the bow.

4. Create-a-Hat - Provide sheets of construction paper, construction paper scraps, scrap materials (buttons, packing "squiggles," pipe cleaners, rickrack, etc.), markers or crayons, scissors, and glue. Direct the children to create an original hat.

5. Headgear Relay - Establish two boundary lines. Divide the class into two even teams. The players on each team place their headgear in a row behind one boundary line and line up single file behind the other. At the signal, the first player on each team runs to the line, puts on his or her headgear, runs back, and tags the next player in line. The relay continues in this manner until all players have participated. The first team to complete the relay wins the game.

Poem - "How Would You Like?"

How would you like to be Peter Pan

And live far away in Never Land?

Where you never grow up and never go to school,

No bedtime, no baths, no spinach, no rules.

How would you like to be Peter Pan

Fighting Captain Hook and his pirate band?

An underground house in which to hide,

And faithful Tinker Bell by your side.

How would you like to be Peter Pan

And live far away in Never Land?

Peter Pan Dramatizations

Divide the class into groups and assign a short scene from the story to each group. Let the groups practice in different areas of the room, then perform the scenes on a designated stage area.

Suggested Scenes:

1. Wendy tells stories of Peter Pan to John and Michael as Nana guards the nursery.

2. Wendy sews Peter Pan's shadow back on as John and Michael watch. Peter Pan tries to convince them to come to Never Land.

3. Peter Pan, Wendy, John, and Michael fly to Never Land. Captain Hook fires cannonballs at them.

4. Tinker Bell, Wendy, John, and Michael slide down the tunnel into Peter Pan's secret house; then they meet the Lost Boys.

5. John, Michael, and the Lost Boys attempt to capture the Indians. Instead, the Indians, disguised as trees, capture them.

6. Captain Hook ties Tiger Lily to Skull Rock. Captain Hook and Peter Pan fight a duel. Peter Pan wins and rescues Tiger Lily.

7. Tinker Bell is captured by Captain Hook and shows him where Peter Pan's house is hidden. Then he locks her in a lantern cage.

8. Captain Hook and his pirates capture Wendy, John, Michael, and the Lost Boys and take them back to the pirate ship. Wendy chooses to walk the plank rather than become a pirate. Peter Pan rescues all of them.

Indian Feathers Color Match

Using the pattern on page 132, make felt feathers of the following colors: red, blue, yellow, green, orange, purple, brown, and black. You should make two of each color for a total of sixteen. Place the feathers in a pile under the flannel board. Put one red feather on the flannel board. Call on a student to identify the color of the feather, then find the other red feather and place it on the flannel board. Repeat with each color. To vary the activity, let a student choose a feather, identify the color, and place it on the flannel board. This student then calls on another student to find the matching feather.

Pirates' Treasure Hunt

For the treasure, purchase chocolate "coins" covered in gold-colored foil, one or two per child. Place in a box. Decide where you want to hide the treasure. You may wish to have the treasure hunt in the school building, on the school grounds, or include both areas. On a crumpled piece of kraft paper, draw a colorful treasure map similar to the example on page 133. For the Treasure Hunt, school rooms become islands, halls become rivers, the flagpole becomes a palm tree, and so forth. Roll up the completed map and tie with string. Hide the "treasure." Tell the children that you have found an ancient pirate's map which leads to a buried treasure. Produce the map, explain it to the "pirates," and begin the Treasure Hunt.

Message in a Bottle

If you live near a large body of water, put a message in an airtight bottle and "send it out to sea." Let the class assist in composing the message and "launching" the bottle. You may wish to attach the message to a self-addressed post card. Then, if it is found, the recipient can write a return message and mail the postcard back to the class.

ART

Peter Pan Caps

Preparation - Purchase paper plates and small elastic. Cut a wedge-shaped piece from each paper plate. Cut elastic into 12" pieces. Mix green tempera paint and set out in aluminum pie pans. Give each child a paper plate, a piece of elastic, and a half-sheet (4½" x 12") of construction paper (any color). Provide paintbrushes, pencils, scissors, staplers, and hole punchers.

Procedure - Paint the back side of the paper plate with the green tempera. While it is drying, draw a feather on the construction paper and cut out. Overlap the two edges of the cut out portion of the paper plate to form a cone shape. Staple. At the bottom of the cap, punch a hole on either side and attach the elastic. Staple the feather above the elastic on one side of the cap. (See example on page 132.)

Your Own Pirate's Flag

Preparation - Mix various colors of tempera paint. Set out along with paintbrushes and pencils. Give each child a sheet of white construction paper or butcher paper. Show the book illustration of Captain Hook's ship. Point out the flag. Tell the children, "Pretend that you are a pirate. Your pirate ship has no flag, so today you will create your own."

Procedure - Think of how you would like your flag to look. Draw, then paint the design. (See example on page 132.)

Note: After the flags have dried, let the children participate in a "show and tell" session with their flags.

Pirate Spyglasses

Preparation - Collect and distribute cardboard paper towel rolls, one per child. Mix tempera paint of various colors. Provide paintbrushes.

Procedure - Paint your spyglass as desired. (See example on page 132.)

MATH

Peter Pan Counting Cap

Duplicate and distribute the sheet on page 134. The students fill in the missing numbers and color the cap.

Indian Chief's Headdress Math Sheet

Duplicate the sheet (page 135) on heavy paper. Distribute. Direct the students to cut out the Indian Chief and the feathers, then match the dots on the feathers with the numbers on the headband. Glue in place. When the glue has dried, the Indian Chief can be colored.

MUSIC - MOVEMENT - GAMES

Song - "Once Upon a Time"

Tune: "Yankee Doodle"

Once upon a time there was
A boy named Peter Pan,
Flew around the friendly skies
And lived in Never Land.

Peter Pan was quite a boy,
Yes he was just dandy,
Super Man to all his friends
And with a sword quite handy.

Songs - "The Second Star to the Right" and "You Can Fly! You Can Fly! You Can Fly!" by Sammy Cahn and Sammy Fain

Source: The Greatest Hits of Walt Disney (LP)

Game - "The Crocodile's Tick Tock" (LP)

Direct the players to stand in a circle. Use a kitchen timer as the crocodile. Set the timer for 1-2 minutes. The players pass the timer around the circle. When the timer rings, the players all shout, "Chop! Chop!" The player holding the ringing timer is "eaten" by the crocodile. This player sits in the middle of the circle and the game resumes. The last player standing is "Peter Pan" and wins the game. If you prefer no eliminations, the player holding the timer when it rings can "swim to safety" (make swimming motions) and remain in the circle. The game will have no winner.

Game - "Peter Pan and the Pirates"

Mark two boundary lines. Divide the class into two groups. One group is "Peter Pan and his Friends." (One player is designated "Peter Pan.") They stand side by side with their backs to one boundary line. The other group, "Captain Hook and his Band of Pirates," stand behind the other boundary line. At the signal, the pirate group sneaks up behind the Peter Pan group. When they are fairly close, Peter Pan says, "Look out! Captain Hook and his pirates!" The Peter Pan group immediately turns around and chases the pirates back to their boundary line. Anyone tagged becomes a member of Peter Pan's group. For the next round, the pirates chase the Peter Pan group.

Game - "Walking the Plank"

Mark off boundaries to be the pirates' ship. All players must remain in this area. One player is chosen to walk the plank. This player is led to the center of the ship, blindfolded, and turned around three times. At this point, the other players scatter within the "ship." The player walking the plank feels his or her way around until he or she finds another player, then says, "I am walking the plank. Will you save me?" The "caught" player, in a disguised voice, replies, "No, no, no!" The player walking the plank has three chances to guess the identity of the "caught" player. If he or she guesses correctly, the "caught" player must walk the plank; if not, that round is over and another child is chosen to walk the plank.

FAIRY TALE KITCHEN

Dinner in Never Land

For Snack Time, plan to serve a typical dinner in Never Land. Brainstorm for menu ideas, reminding the class about the nature of Never Land (no parents, no rules, etc.). Try to keep the menu simple so that the class may participate in the preparations as much as possible.

Sample Ideas:

"Main Course" - Peanut Butter and Jelly or Baloney or Ham and Cheese (Finger) Sandwiches
Drinks - Soft Drinks
Vegetables - Corn Chips and Bean Dip or Potato Chips and Onion Dip
Fruits - Fig Newtons, Fruit-flavored Candy
Bread - Donuts, Muffins
Dessert - Banana Splits

Dear Parents,

On _____, our class will share the fairy tale "Peter Pan."
The day's lessons and activities will center around this fairy tale. Please
read below for ways you can help.

Things to send: _____

_____

_____

Volunteers needed to: _____

_____

_____

Follow-up Activities: Ask your child to share the following songs,
games, and other activities related to the fairy
tale:

_____

_____

_____

Ask your child the following questions about the fairy tale:

_____

_____

_____

Thank you for your cooperation.

Sincerely,

Dear Parents,

On _____, our class will share the fairy tale "Peter Pan." In conjunction with the story, we will also have "Happy Headgear Day."

In the story, the characters wear a variety of headgear. Peter Pan wears a small cap with a feather, Captain Hook wears a huge wide-brimmed hat, John wears a top hat, Wendy wears a bow, the Indians wear headdresses, and so forth. For our "Happy Headgear Day," we will have several activities centering around this theme; therefore, I am asking that your child wear his or her favorite headgear (cap, hat, etc.) to school. Please label your child's headgear with his or her name.

Thank you for your cooperation.

Sincerely,

Dear Parents,

Just a reminder that tomorrow is "Happy Headgear Day." Please let your child wear his or her favorite headgear to school. Thank you.

Sincerely,

Headgear Day. Patterns

Headgear Day. Patterns

Pattern, Examples

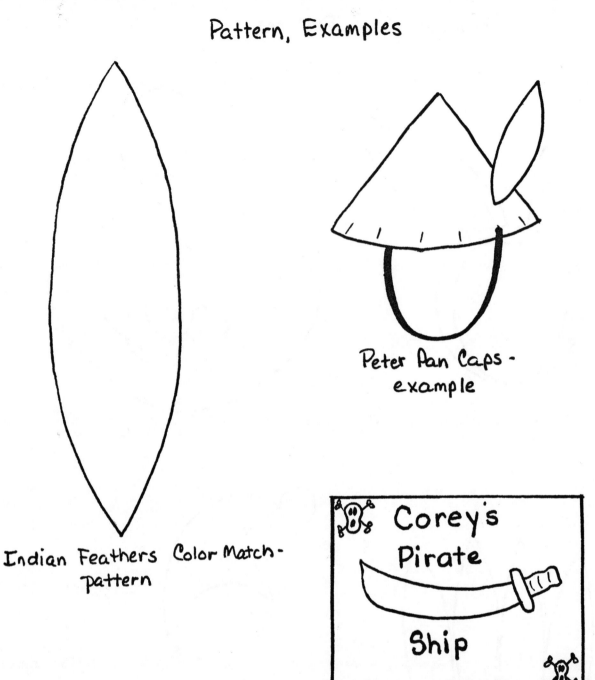

Indian Feathers Color Match-
pattern

Peter Pan Caps -
example

Your Own Pirate's Flag -
example

Pirate Spyglasses
example

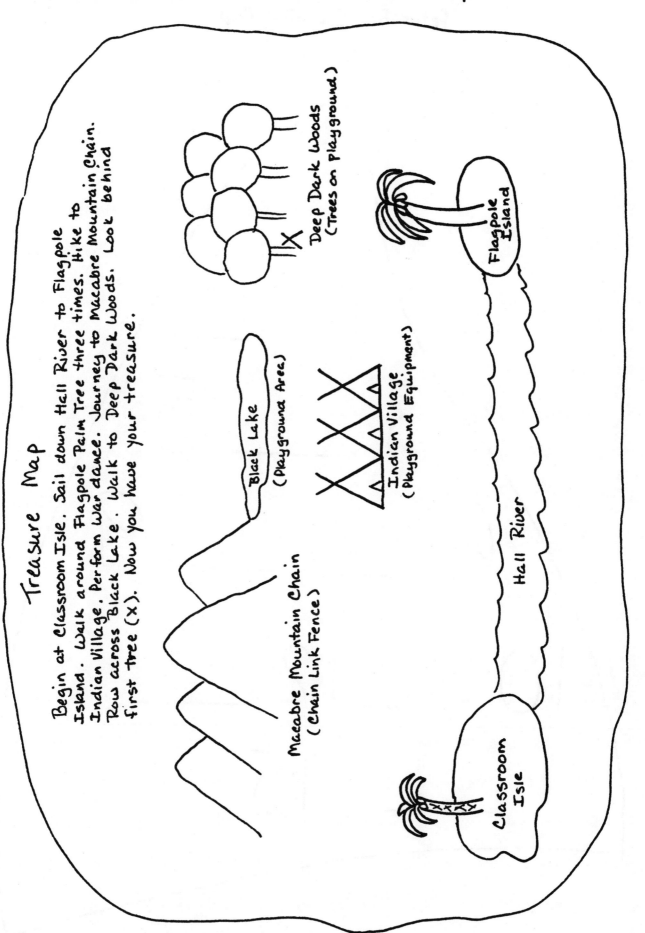

Treasure Map

Begin at Classroom Isle. Sail down Hall River to Flagpole Island. Walk around Flagpole Palm Tree three times. Hike to Indian Village. Perform war dance. Journey to Macabre Mountain Chain. Row across Black Lake. Walk to Deep Dark Woods. Look behind first tree (X). Now you have your treasure.

Deep Dark Woods
(Trees on Playground)

Flagpole Island

Black Lake
(Playground Area)

Indian Village
(Playground Equipment)

Macabre Mountain Chain
(Chain Link Fence)

Hall River

Classroom Isle

Peter Pan Counting Cap

Indian Chief's Headdress Math Sheet

THE WOLF AND THE SEVEN KIDS

Source: <u>The Wolf and the Seven Kids</u> by the Brothers Grimm, illustrated by Kinuko Y. Craft (Troll Associates)

LANGUAGE ARTS - SOCIAL STUDIES - SCIENCE

Before the Story

Send home the parents' letter on page 143, if desired. Duplicate the Student's Tell-a-Story patterns on pages 144 and 145. Distribute along with one 3½" x 6½" white envelope per child. Set out scissors, crayons, and glue. Direct the children to seal the envelopes and cut off one narrow end, color and cut out the patterns, then glue the wolf on the front of the envelope. (The wolf's head should be above the cut end of the envelope.) Set these aside until after the story.

Copy the Paper Bag patterns as directed on page 146. Color and cut out. Glue the wolf's face at the top of a paper bag. Set the paper bag, the paper "kids," a handful of rocks, a pair of scissors, and scotch tape on the Display Table.

Read the story. When the wolf eats the kids, place them in the paper bag and tape the top. When the mother cuts open the wolf, use the scissors to cut a slit in the paper bag and remove the "kids." Next, put the rocks in the paper bag and "sew it" closed with scotch tape. Drop the bag on the floor when the wolf falls in the well.

Vocabulary Words

nanny goat	cupboard	stones
kids	grandfather clock	well
hoarse	meadow	balance
miller	weeping	

After the Story

The children hold their "wolf envelopes" and place the other Tell-a-Story patterns nearby. Reread the story or let the children take turns telling the story. The children hold up the different characters as they are mentioned, and, at the proper places in the story, fill up the "wolf envelope" with six of the kids, then empty it and fill it with the paper stones.

Discuss the story and how the characters felt in the different situations. Brainstorm for "Rules to Follow When You Are Home Alone" and list on the board.

Kid and Mother Pathtracer

Duplicate and distribute the sheet on page 147. The students trace the path from the kid to his mother.

Knock, Knock, Who's There? - Listening Game

Choose one player to be the "Kid." The "Kid" sits in a chair with his or her back to the class and closes his or her eyes. Point to another player. This player walks up behind the "Kid" and knocks on the back of the chair. The "Kid" says "Who's there?" and the player, in a disguised voice, says, "It is your mother." The "Kid" then tries to guess the player's identity saying, "No, you're not, you are _____ (child's name)." If the "Kid" is correct, he or she gets to remain in the chair. If the "Kid" is incorrect, the player becomes the new "Kid."

Rhyme - Hickory Dickory Dock, The Kid Hid in the Clock" (adapted from Mother Goose)

Teach the following rhyme. As the children recite the rhyme, hit a cooking pot with a spoon (the correct number of times) when the clock strikes in each verse. Repeat the rhyme and let the children use rhythm instruments to imitate the clock striking.

Hickory dickory dock,
The kid hid in the clock;
The clock struck one;
The kid's ears rung,
Hickory dickory dock.

Hickory dickory dock,
The kid hid in the clock;
The clock struck two;
The kid turned blue,
Hickory dickory dock.

Hickory dickory dock,
The kid hid in the clock;
The clock stuck three;
The kid cried, "Gee,"
Hickory dickory dock.

Hickory dickory dock,
The kid hid in the clock;
The clock struck four;
He could take no more,
Hickory dickory dock.

Hickory dickory dock,
The kid beat up the clock;
It hit the floor,
And struck no more,
Hickory dickory dock.

Initial Sounds Activity

Use pellon to make the patterns on pages 148 through 151. Color with crayons. One at a time, place the groups listed below on the flannel board. Call on students to identify the three items; then ask the students to identify the item which begins with a different sound than the other two. Continue in this manner with each group of items.

1. door, car, cake
2. grapes, stones, grass
3. house, haystack, clock
4. book, pencil, pot
5. duck, wolf, donut

Variation: Make a copy of the patterns, color, cut out, and glue on tagboard squares. Place three squares at a time on the chalkboard ledge or on a clothesline constructed for this purpose. Follow the identification procedure as described above.

ART

Kid in the Clock

Preparation - Cut a 3" x 12" piece of white construction paper for each child. Distribute. Provide crayons or markers. Draw a simple grandfather clock on the chalkboard and/or show the grandfather clock in the book's illustrations. Also, demonstrate different easy methods of drawing a kid.

Procedure - Fold the piece of construction paper in half to measure 6" x 3" and place in front of you with the fold at the top. This will be the grandfather clock. Draw the face, etc., and color. Unfold the clock and draw the kid inside. (See examples on page 152.)

Wolf Sewing Cards

Preparation - Duplicate the wolf (see page 153) on white construction paper. Cut 9" pieces of yarn. Distribute the patterns and yarn. Set out crayons, scissors, and hole punchers.

Procedure - Cut out and color the wolf. Punch holes on the dots. Tie one end of the yarn to the first hole. Use the other end as a "needle" and "sew up" the wolf by going in and out of the holes. When you have finished, let the teacher tie and knot the end to the last hole. (See example on page 152.)

Variation: Pebbles may be glued on the wolf's stomach, if desired.

Clay Wells

Preparation - Purchase self-hardening clay and black chenille pipe cleaners. Cut the pipe cleaners into 3" or 4" pieces. Give each child enough clay to make a small well, a pipe cleaner piece, and a toothpick. The children may use the pinch pot method or coil method described below.

Procedure (1) - (Pinch Pot Method) - Roll the clay into a ball and make an indentation in the center. Mold into the shape of a well (cylinder). Use the toothpicks to draw the bricks on the outside of the well. Dry. Curl the pipe cleaner piece and position over the side of the well to represent the wolf's tail.

Procedure (2) - (Coil Method) - Roll the clay into a long rope. Coil the rope into a circle to form the base of the well, then coil around and around to form the sides of the well. Wet your fingers and smooth together the coils on the inside of the well. With the toothpick, make vertical lines on the outside coils to represent the bricks. Dry. Place the pipe cleaner tail over the side as described above (in Procedure 1). (See examples on page 152.)

MATH

Rocks in a Jar

Make a copy of the wolf on page 144 or 151, depending on the size of the jar. Cut out and glue to the front of a jar. Fill the jar with rocks. Turn the jar around so the students can see the rocks and ask them to guess how many rocks are in the jar. Write the guesses on the chalkboard. Let the students assist in opening the jar and counting the rocks. Write the total on the chalkboard. Compare the total with the students' guesses.

Hiding the Kids - Positions Sheet

Duplicate and distribute the sheet on page 154. Give the following directions:

1. Draw a kid under the table.
2. Draw a kid in the bed.
3. Draw a kid inside the oven.
4. Draw a kid in the kitchen.
5. Draw a kid over the cupboard.
6. Draw a kid under the sink.
7. Draw a kid inside the grandfather clock.

Note: The kids can be drawn as simple stick figures.

MUSIC - MOVEMENT - GAMES

Song - "Oh, the Wolf"

Tune: "If You're Happy and You Know It

Oh, the wolf found the kids and ate them up,

Oh, the wolf found the kids and ate them up,

Oh, the wolf found the kids,

Oh, the wolf found the kids,

Oh, the wolf found the kids and ate them up.

But another kid was hidden in the clock,

But another kid was hidden in the clock,

But another kid was hidden,

But another kid was hidden,

But another kid was hidden in the clock.   (Ate them up)

Oh, the mother found the wolf and cut 'em out,

Oh, the mother found the wolf and cut 'em out,

Oh, the mother found the wolf,

Oh, the mother found the wolf,

Oh, the mother found the wolf and cut 'em out.   (In the clock,
ate them up)

Oh, the kids got some stones and filled him up,

Oh, the kids got some stones and filled him up,

Oh, the kids got some stones,

Oh, the kids got some stones,

Oh, the kids got some stones and filled him up,   (Cut 'em out,
in the clock, ate them up)

Oh, the wolf fell in the well and that was that,

Oh, the wolf fell in the well and that was that,

Oh, the wolf fell in the well,

Oh, the wolf fell in the well,

Oh, the wolf fell in the well and that was that.   (Filled him up,
cut 'em out, in the clock, ate them up)

Game - "Tossing Stones"

Make a well from a corrugated cardboard box. Mark a throwing line and divide the class into two or more teams. Using three tennis balls or beanbags, each player tries to toss the "stones" into the well. A successful toss results in one point scored for the player's team. Play for a certain amount of time or until one team reaches a predetermined amount of points.

Outside Game - "You're Not Our Mother, You're Another"

Mark two goal lines thirty to forty feet apart. One player is the "Wolf" and stands in the center between the two goal lines. The rest of the players are the "Kids" and stand behind one of the goal lines.

The "Wolf" shouts, "Knock, knock, Kids!"
The "Kids" shout, "Who's there?"
The "Wolf" answers, "It's your mother!"
The "Kids" shout, "You're not our mother, you're another!"

At this point, the "Kids" must run from one goal to the other with the "Wolf" attempting to tag them. Those tagged must join hands with the "Wolf." For the next round, the procedure is repeated, but this time the previously tagged players must continue holding hands with the "Wolf" and try to tag the "Kids." Only the end players may actually tag a "Kid." As a "Kid" is tagged, he or she joins the chain. If the chain breaks, all the "Kids" tagged (in that round) are released. The game continues until all "Kids" are tagged.

FAIRY TALE KITCHEN

Edible Stone Cookies

3/4 cup butter or margarine
1 1/2 cups sugar
3 eggs
2 cups flour
1 1/2 teaspoons cinnamon
1/8 cup boiling water
1 teaspoon soda
2 cups raisins
2 cups pecans

Preheat oven to 400°. Mix the soda with the boiling water. Cream butter and sugar. Add eggs and mix well. Add flour, cinnamon, boiling water and soda to the butter, sugar, and egg mixture. Mix well; then add raisins and pecans. Drop by heaping teaspoonfuls, 2" apart, on a lightly greased cookie sheet. Bake 10-15 minutes or until light brown. Yield: 6 dozen cookies

Dear Parents,

On _____, our class will share the fairy tale "The Wolf and the Seven Kids." The day's lessons and activities will center around this fairy tale. Please read below for ways you can help.

Things to send: _____
_____
_____

Volunteers needed to: _____
_____
_____

Follow-up Activities: Ask your child to share the following songs, games, and other activities related to the fairy tale:

_____
_____
_____

Ask your child the following questions about the fairy tale:

_____
_____
_____

Thank you for your cooperation.

Sincerely,

Student's Tell-a-Story Patterns

Student's Tell-a-Story Patterns

make
- 1 copy

make
- 1 copy

- make ten copies

make 7 copies

The Wolf and the Seven Kids - Paper Bag Patterns

Make one copy
of wolf.

Make six copies of
the kid. Color the
vest of each kid
a different color.

Kid and Mother Pathtracer

Trace the path from the kid to his mother.

Name _____

Initial Sounds Activity
Patterns

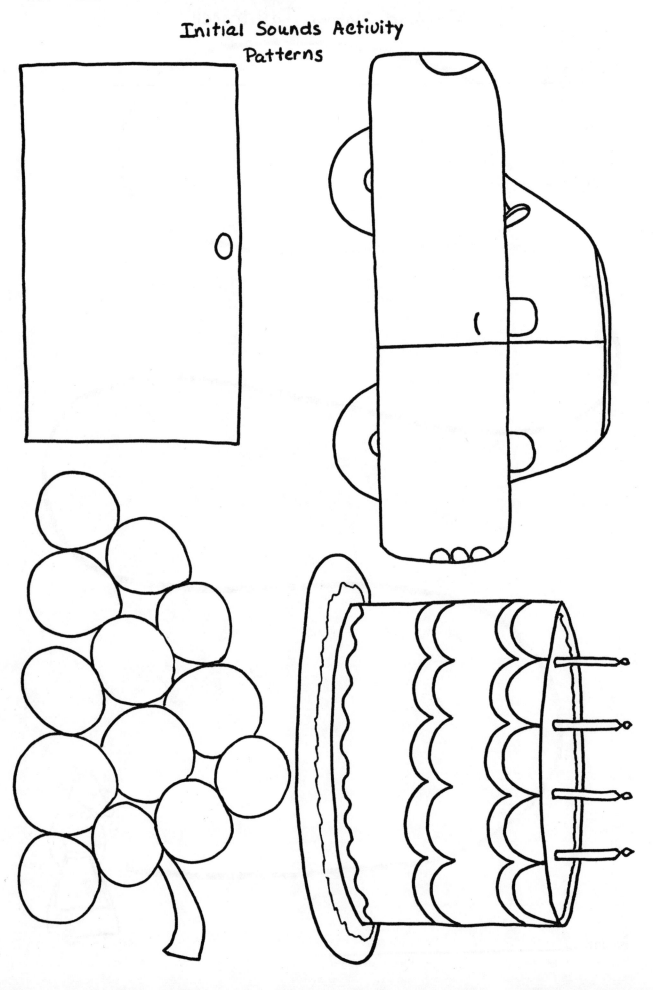

Initial Sounds Activity
Patterns

Initial Sounds Activity
Patterns

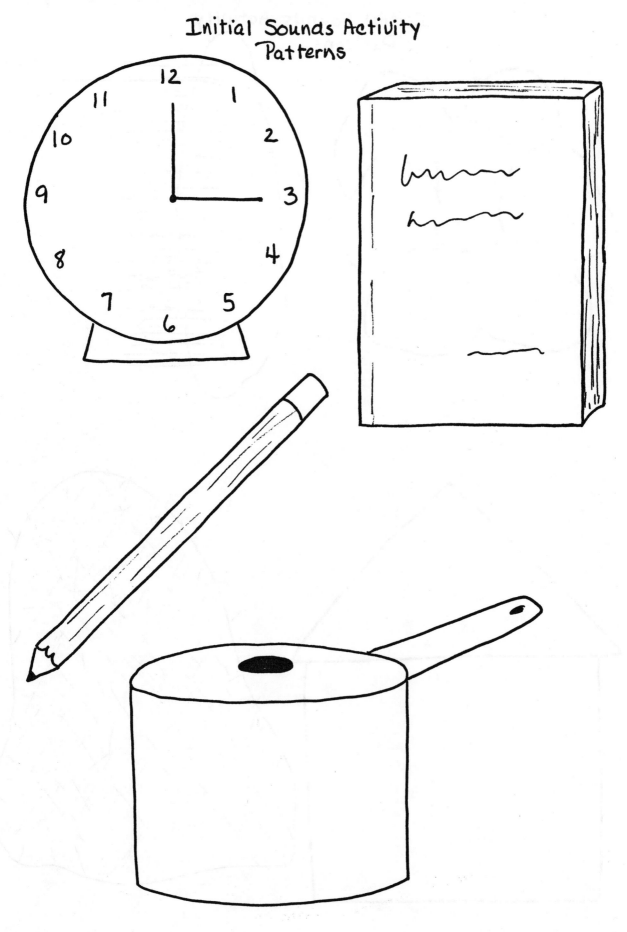

Initial Sounds Activity
Patterns

Examples

Outside
View

Kid in the Clock

Inside
View —

← fold

Wolf Sewing Cards

Clay Wells

Pinch Pot Method

Coil Method

Wolf Sewing Cards

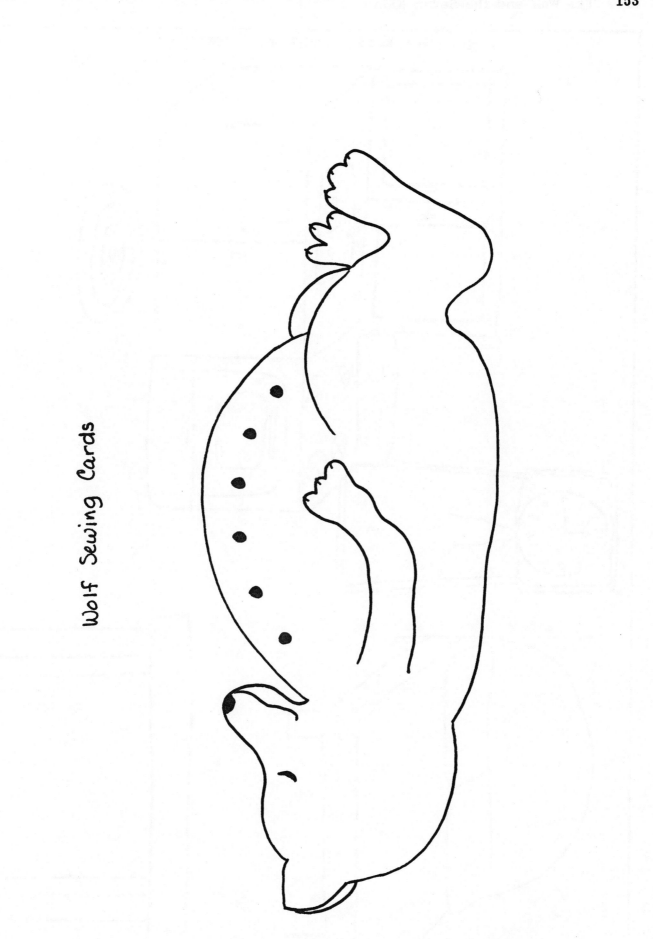

Hiding the Kids - Positions Sheet

BIBLIOGRAPHY

Cavendish, Marshall. <u>My Big Book of Fairy Tales</u>. New York: Exeter Books, 1987.

Disney, Walt. <u>Peter Pan</u>. Racine, Wisconsin: Western Publishing Co., 1987.

Disney, Walt. <u>The Wonderful World of Walt Disney: Fantasyland</u>. New York: Golden Press, 1965.

Grimm, Jacob and Wilhelm. <u>Hansel and Gretel</u>. New York: Delacorte Press, 1971.

Grimm, Jacob and Wilhelm. <u>Little Red Riding Hood</u>. New York: Harcourt, Brace and World, Inc., 1968.

Grimm, Jacob and Wilhelm. <u>The Wolf and the Seven Kids</u>. Mahwah, New Jersey: Troll Associates, 1979.

Ross, Tony. <u>Jack and the Beanstalk</u>. New York: Delacorte Press, 1980.

Alphabet Circus Train, 68, 82
Alphabet Picture Necklace, 68, 82
And He Climbed and He Climbed
    and He Climbed, choral poem, 56
And They Lived Happily Ever After,
    bulletin board, 2, 9
Apple Activity, 41
Apple Trees, math, 44, 53
Apples, Baked, 45
Apples, Padded Poison, 43, 49-50
Arranging Flowers, Activity and
    Sheet, 14, 26

Backdrop, Story Area, 1, 4
Baked Apples, 45
Bean Mosaics, 58, 65
Bear Counting Booklet, 105,
    113-119
Bear Went Over the Mountain, The,
    song, 106
Bears, Fingerpainted, 105, 111
Bibbidi-Bobbidi-Boo, 91
Big News, action story, 69
Big/Middle-Sized/Small Sheet,
    105, 120
Bulletin Boards, 2

Cakes, Tiny Apple, 15
Caps For Sale, 122
Ceiling Decorations, 1
Ceiling Decorations, patterns, 5
Character Role-Playing, 87
Character Shout, 28
Chin Skit, 102, 109
Cinderella Parents' Letter, 93
Cinderella, After the Story, 86
Cinderella, Before the Story, 86
Cinderella, song, 90
Cinderella, Unit, 86
Cinderella, Vocabulary Words, 86
Cinderella's Coach, 88, 96-97
Cinderella's Glass Slipper, 89,
    97, 99
Circus Activities, movement, 74
Circus Painting, 72, 82
Clay Wells, art, 139, 152
Clifford, the Big Red Dog, 11
Climbing the Beanstalk, Wall
    Display, 1, 6
Clock Search, game, 91
Count the Peanuts, math, 72
Counting Rhyme, 58
Create-a-Hat, 122

Crocodile's Tick Tock, The, game,
    126

Dance With the Ugly Stepsister,
    game, 91
Dancing Dwarfs, 45
Days of the Week Elephants, 70,
    79-80
Decorations, Ceiling, 1
Decorations, Ceiling, patterns, 5
Dialogue Tape, 121
Dinner in Never Land, 127
Disney's Children's Favorites,
    Volume II (LP), 106
Display Table, 1
Display, Wall, Climbing the
    Beanstalk, 1, 6
Displays, 1
Do Your Ears Hang Low?, 74
Dumbo Color Sheet, 71, 81
Dumbo Finger Puppets, 71, 82, 84
Dumbo Flannel Board Patterns,
    77-78
Dumbo Masks, 71, 82-83
Dumbo of the Circus Parents'
    Letter, 76
Dumbo of the Circus, 67
Dumbo of the Circus, After the
    Story, 67
Dumbo of the Circus, Before the
    Story, 67
Dumbo of the Circus, Unit, 67
Dumbo of the Circus, Vocabulary
    Words, 67
Dumbo the Elephant, art, 82
Dumbo the Flying Elephant, art,
    72, 85
Dumbo, song, 73,
Dumbo's Booklet of Opposites,
    math, 72
Dumbo's Favorite Peanut Butter
    Candy, 75

Edible Stone Cookies, 142
Elephants, Days of the Week, 70,
    79-80

Fairy Tale Fun, bulletin board
    pattern, 7
Fairy Tale Fun, bulletin board,
    2, 8
Fee Fie Fo Fum, song, 60
Feeding the Elephants, game, 75

Filling the Wolf with Stones, math, 13, 25

Fingerpainted Bears, 105, 111

Flannel Board Activity, How Do They Feel?, 29

Following Directions Activity, 122

Gingerbread House Number Puzzle, 31, 39-40

Gingerbread Houses, 29, 36

Gingerbread, 32

Going to Grandma's, Alphabet Game and Follow-Up, 12, 20

Going to Grandma's, Alphabet Gameboard, 19

Goldilocks and the Bear, game, 106

Goldilocks and the Three Bears Parents' Letter, 108

Goldilocks and the Three Bears Peep Boxes, 105, 112

Goldilocks and the Three Bears, After the Story, 102

Goldilocks and the Three Bears, Before the Story, 102

Goldilocks and the Three Bears, fingerplay, 104

Goldilocks and the Three Bears, Unit, 102

Goldilocks and the Three Bears, Vocabulary Words, 102

Goldilocks, 102

Grandma's Garb, game, 15

Greatest Hits of Walt Disney, The, (LP), 44, 74, 91, 126

Hansel and Gretel Alphabet Activity, 28

Hansel and Gretel Parents' Letter, 33

Hansel and Gretel, 27

Hansel and Gretel, After the Story, 27

Hansel and Gretel, alphabet activity, 34

Hansel and Gretel, Before the Story, 27

Hansel and Gretel, dance, 31

Hansel and Gretel, Demonstration, 28

Hansel and Gretel, recording, 31

Hansel and Gretel, Unit, 27

Hansel and Gretel, Vocabulary Words, 27

Hansel's Prison, art, 30, 36

Happy Headgear Day Parents' Letter, 129

Happy Headgear Day, 122, 130-131

Hard and Soft Sheet, 103, 110

He'll Be Climbin' Down the Beanstalk, song, 59

Headgear Day, Happy, 122, 130-131

Headgear Day, Happy, Parents' Letter, 129

Headgear Relay, 123

Heigh Ho, Heigh Ho, 44

Hickory Dickory Dock, The Kid Hid in the Clock, 137

Hiding the Kids, Positions Sheet, 140, 154

How Do They Feel?, flannel board activity, 29, 35

How Would You Like?, poem, 123

Hungry Wolf, The, 13, 20, 24

I Like Red, 10

I Spy, game, 11

"I'm a Giant" Walking Cans, 57, 65

Indian Chief's Headdress Math Sheet, 126, 135

Indian Feathers Color Match, 124, 132

Initial Sounds Activity, 138, 148-151

Jack and the Beanstalk Live Mural, 54, 63

Jack and the Beanstalk Parents' Letter, 62

Jack and the Beanstalk, 54

Jack and the Beanstalk, After the Story, 54

Jack and the Beanstalk, Before the Story, 54

Jack and the Beanstalk, Unit, 54

Jack and the Beanstalk, Vocabulary Words, 54

Jack and the Giant, game, 61

Jack on the Beanstalk, art, 57, 65

Jack's Beanstalks, recipe, 61

Kid and Mother Pathtracer, 137, 147

Kid in the Clock, art, 139, 152

Knock, Knock, Who's There, Listening Game,   137

Learning Basic Skills Through Music, Volume I,   74
Listening Cans,   57
Little Cottage in the Wood, song,   106
Little Gray Elephant, A, fingerplay,   70
Little Red Caboose, song,   11
Little Red Riding Hood Maze,   12, 18
Little Red Riding Hood Parents' Letter,   16
Little Red Riding Hood,   10
Little Red Riding Hood, After the Story,   10
Little Red Riding Hood, Before the Story,   10
Little Red Riding Hood, Unit,   10
Little Red Riding Hood, Vocabulary Words,   10
Little Red Riding Hood's Tale, fingerplay,   11

Me, Oh, My, choral poem,   86
Mean and Hungry People-Eater, song,   14
Measuring Activities,   58
Measuring Sheet,   66
Message in a Bottle,   124
Mirror Activities,   43
Mirror Movements,   45
Mouse Cookies,   92
My Big Book of Fairy Tales,   102

Name the Seven Dwarfs,   42
Name the Seven Dwarfs, Follow-Up Sheet,   48
Nibble, Nibble, game,   31

Oh, the Wolf, song,   140
On the Beanstalk, movement,   60
Once Upon a Time, song,   126

Padded Poison Apples,   43, 49-50
Pairs Sheet,   90, 101
Paper Weave Baskets,   13, 20, 23
Peanut Butter,   75
Peanut Drop, game,   75
Peanut Toss, game,   75

Pease-Porridge Hot, clapping rhyme,   103
Pebble Walk, game,   32
Peter Pan and the Pirates, game,   127
Peter Pan Caps,   125, 132
Peter Pan Counting Cap,   125, 134
Peter Pan Dramatizations,   123
Peter Pan Parents' Letter,   128
Peter Pan, After the Story,   122
Peter Pan, Before the Story,   121
Peter Pan, Unit,   121
Peter Pan, Vocabulary Words,   121
Pirate Spyglasses,   125, 132
Pirates' Treasure Hunt,   124, 133
Planting Seeds Activity,   55
Poison Apple, game,   45
Porridge and Fruit,   107
Porridge Eating Contest,   106
Prop Box,   2
Pumpkin Math,   89
Pumpkin Seeds, Toasted,   92
Pumpkin, Seeds in, math,   90
Pumpkins, Pumpkins,   88
Pumpkins, Seeds in, math,   100

Red Day Parents' Letter,   17
Red Day,   10
Rhyming Words,   27, 122
Rocks in a Jar, math,   140
Room Environment,   1
Rooms in the House Activity,   103
Run Away, Run Away, song,   31

Second Star to the Right, The,   126
Seeds in the Pumpkin, math,   90, 100
Sequence of a Pumpkin's Growth, cards,   88, 95
Shapes Mouse,   89, 97-98
Snow White and the Seven Dwarfs Mural,   43, 49
Snow White and the Seven Dwarfs Parents' Letter,   47
Snow White and the Seven Dwarfs, After the Story,   41
Snow White and the Seven Dwarfs, Before the Story,   41
Snow White and the Seven Dwarfs, Unit,   41

Snow White and the Seven Dwarfs, Vocabulary Words, 41
Snow White Counting Sheet, 44, 52
Snow White's Presents, action game, 42
Spilling the Beans Game, 59
Stick Puppets, Snow White and the Seven Dwarfs, 44, 51
Story Area Backdrop, 1, 4, 102
Story Telling Beanstalk, 54, 63
Student's Tell-a-Story Patterns, 136, 144-145

Table, Display, 1
Things That Fly, Things That Swim, 71
Things That Go Together, sheet, 56, 64
Time Activities, 87
Time Sheet, 94
Tiny Apple Cakes, 15
Toasted Pumpkin Seeds, 92
Tossing Stones, game, 141
Trail to Grandma's, footprint, 20
Trail to Grandma's, movement, 14

Visual Discrimination Activity, 11

Walking the Plank, game, 127
Wall Display, Climbing the Beanstalk, 1, 6
Walt Disney's Cinderella, 86
Walt Disney's Fantasyland, 67
Walt Disney's Peter Pan, 121
Walt Disney's Snow White And The Seven Dwarfs, 41

Wee Sing Silly Songs, 74, 106
What's Missing, 104
When I See an Elephant Fly, song, 74
When You Wish Upon a Star, bulletin board, 2, 9
Whistle While You Work, 44
Witch's Jewels, The, math, 30, 38
Wolf and the Seven Kids Paper Bag Patterns, The, 136, 146
Wolf and the Seven Kids Parents' Letter, The, 143
Wolf and the Seven Kids, The, 136
Wolf and the Seven Kids, The, After the Story, 136
Wolf and the Seven Kids, The, Before the Story, 136
Wolf and the Seven Kids, The, Unit, 136
Wolf and the Seven Kids, The, Vocabulary Words, 136
Wolf Sewing Cards, 139, 152-153
Wolf, The Hungry, 20, 24
Wolf, The Hungry, art, 13
Wolf's X-Rays, The, 12, 20-22
Woodcutter's Axe, art, 30, 36-37

You Can Fly! You Can Fly! You Can Fly!, 126
You're Not Our Mother, You're Another, outside game, 142
Your Own Pirate's Flag, 125, 132